THE NOBLE
CHAIN

MICHAEL BASSEY ENEYO

Published by Harmony Publishing

Plot 1 Emmanuel Anabor, Off Mopo Road, United Estate, Sangotedo, Lagos, Nigeria

+2347032212481

publish@harmonypublishing.com.ng

ISBN: 978-1-0056-5546-4

Printed in Nigeria

This book is dedicated to all workers in Kitoto for their contributions to the growth of the state, especially teachers whose profession is noble, yet, are constantly in the chains of suffering and financial limitations.

iv

Acknowledgements

Acknowledging someone's efforts and contributions is a motivation to spur the person to do more. Therefore, I would like to take this moment to appreciate some individuals who have contributed in ways that cannot be quantified to make life more desirable and worth living.

My sincere appreciation goes to teachers all over the world for their contributions to the laying of solid foundations for people to study and understand the world better. I specially thank all the lecturers in the Department of Philosophy, University of Calabar, Nigeria, for making the department one of the best to be reckoned with in Nigeria and in the world at large.

There are people whose contributions to the success of this book can never be undermined. Let me at this point acknowledge Dr. (Barr.) John Edor, the ASUU Chairman, University of Calabar branch, for creating time to write the foreword of this book; I'm grateful sir. I humbly acknowledge AC, R.T. Shaahu, my much respected boss and mentor; thank you sir for your contributions. Chief Dr. Emeka Okonkwo (E-Money); your contributions to the development of the youths can never go unnoticed. It is always a noble act to appreciate people who have chosen the path of helping others, especially those that are weighed down by the bad administrative system of a state despite their earnest struggles. It is on this note that the name; Obinna Iyiegbu, popularly known as OBI CUBANA comes to mind. Sir, for your contributions in helping many of the youths in the state to overcome the geography of their financial and poverty limitations; may God keep blessing you. SC Y.A Adamu, officers and the entire staff of the Emy Cargo Terminal, I pray God bless you all for your support.

To the entire Officers and Men of the Nigeria Customs Service, I can't thank you enough for providing me with an enabling environment to utilize my writing potential.

Let me at this point specially acknowledge my dear wife, Dr. Mrs. Violet Eneyo, my children: Oniong,

Abasi-Ekong, and Ase-Abasi; you remain my source of motivation. I love you.

And, finally, to God, the giver of all good things for seeing me through in putting the fragmented ideas together. Thank you Lord.

Michael Bassey Eneyo

Table of Contents

x

Foreword

By ontological determinism, and by cosmetical manipulations, wo/man is condemned to being in chains. The thesis of the phantasmagoria of freedom underscores the entire corpus of Michael Bassey Eneyo's book: The Noble Chain. The requirements of nature, compounded by existential necessities, appear to have irredeemably placed wo/man in a position where her/his "choices" are sufficiently limited. Michael Bassey Eneyo expounds the doctrines of natural law, and wo/man-made law in this book. While conceding to the fact that wo/man is no less constrained by natural designs in her/his actions, the book The Noble Chain laments the regrettable situation where wo/man-made chains and yoke are deliberately imposed upon the society. Every human society is saturated with customs, rules, principles, traditions, laws, ethics, etiquette, and norms that regulate transactions, dealings, and interactions with one another. This cluster of aforementioned requirements is what is referred to herein as wo/man-made chains. These cultural requirements are actually meant to make human relations easier, since by nature, human interests are variegated. However, in the State of Kitoto – a fictitious name for Nigeria – because of the level of mental development of both the leaders and the led of Kitoto, the citizens have saturated themselves with foreign cultural norms, which are suffocating them because the foreign norms are uncongenial with the cultural space of the State of Kitoto. But most fundamentally, the purveyors of these foreign-imposed norms and traditions have no altruistic motives, as their covert intention is the expropriation and looting of both the natural and human resources found in the State of Kitoto. The author herein refers to them, for good reasons, as golden vultures. Both for religious and material assets, Michael Bassey Eneyo warns very sternly that the citizens of the State of Kitoto need to be wary of foreign impositions, for a vulture simply comes to devour.

The primary focus of the book The Noble Chain is the education sector of the State of Kitoto. The author canvasses the position, and correctly so, that education is the bedrock of development in any society. In the State of Kitoto (remember it is a euphemism for Nigeria), the leaders have jettisoned and relegated education to an item of little or no priority. Most of Kitoto's leaders barely have significant education. In fact, it is even the law of the land as enshrined in the grundnorm of the land, and as interpreted by the apex court, that leadership does not require much education. This perception of education by the leaders of the State of Kitoto is an anti-thesis to the need for quality and supreme education for leaders as espoused in The Republic of Plato, the originators of democracy, which the State of Kitoto pretends to practice.

In the State of Kitoto, because of the insignificant value attached to education, the sector is practically comatose. Children of the rich are not sent to public schools in the State of Kitoto, because their parents know that the schools are not in a good state. The libraries are archaic, and while the laboratories are empty, the lecture theatres are infested with rodents and reptiles. The staffers in the public schools are paupers and walking corpses (represented in the character of Akana in the book, and though the teaching profession is a noble one, the teacher in the State of Kitoto is in a chain – The Noble Chain), and there is a general infrastructural decay in public schools. No parent who can afford quality education outside the State of Kitoto, or in a private institution within the State of Kitoto, would wish to send her/his child to Kitoto's public schools.

Michael Bassey Eneyo, like many other Nigerians – the author of this book is a Nigerian – sincerely yearns for the liberation of the soul of education from the shackles of leadership oppression. He identifies two basic reasons why the incessant struggles by the teachers unions in the State of Kitoto have not yielded results: insincerity and lack of commitment on the part of political leaders in the State of Kitoto, and the attitude of the leaders of the teachers unions in the State of Kitoto. It is really regrettable that education is being trifled with by leaders of this society, it is unfortunate and pathetic. Michael Bassey Eneyo calls for a total liberation of the teacher in the State of Kitoto from the chains of pauperism, compromise, and by tackling dearth of infrastructure, and improved working conditions.

I sincerely commend this author for his bravery and courage. I commend him for finding time to go into publishing, for this is among his numerous books, in spite of being a public servant in a non-education sector. I commend the author for exposing the laxity on the part of our leaders to prioritise education. This book is easy to read and comprehend, as the author has presented his arguments in a very simple fashion.

Edor J. Edor PhD

Philosophy Department, University of Calabar, Calabar,

ASUU Chairman, University of Calabar Chapter, Cross River State, Nigeria.

Introduction

To be in chains is typical of every human being on earth. Some chains are natural, while some are made by humans. These chains manifest in different forms in our lives. Some manifest in the form of laws, rules, and constitutions we make to guide our actions as a people. While others are embedded in the culture, custom, ethics, and norms, we observe in our daily lives. Again, a chain can manifest in the jobs or businesses we engage in. These various chains place limitations and constraints on us from doing those things we may ordinarily have done if there were no such limitations in the name of rules, guides, or laws. Also, the chain we find ourselves in can result from the kind of relationship we keep. Such chains can deter us from achieving our respective goals if the rules guiding the job or such relationship are not made to protect the interest of all.

The chain engulfing us determines the extent we can go in life. To go far, you must choose a chain that will not hold down your dreams. You cannot go to engineering school to become a nurse. Engineering school only qualifies you to be an engineer. An herbalist must know the functions of some herbs. This is not so with someone that is studying law in school. A farmer is expected to take care of the farm, just as the carpenter must know how to join wood with wood. These are the kind of chains, or let me say laws, that are associated with our careers, in which we must steadfastly follow if we must succeed. Making this choice means we have chosen the kind of chains [laws} we want to surrender ourselves to. It is essential to understand the kind of man-made chain we embrace; else, we may never live to actualize our dreams. Every society has its respective chains (laws). Family, marriage, contract, school, and so on, are the different chains that humans find themselves leashed with. Right from when we were born, our human nature has been to be in chain.

No matter our level in the society or the achievement, we are all somewhat leashed with chains {laws}. Whether you are a leader or the subject, none is entirely free from stipulated rules which are chains.

The leader is obliged to lead according to the rules, while the subject is expected to obey the laws. Irrespective of the perspective we may be looking at, none of them is actually free from chain. Most times we are deceived to think we are free, but this is far from the truth.

Jean Rousseau in his "Social Contract" had said that "man is born free and everywhere he is in chains." In the epistemic frame, the assertion is a half-truth, if there is anything like that. No man is born free, as Rousseau wants us to believe. The natural delivery of every child is necessitated by the conception by a woman. This must also be at the instance of a man. Even in this technological and the artificial intelligent period, any of such manipulations to create human beings must be technologically necessitated. This makes freedom an illusion in the real sense of the word.

The universe is a proof of human's entanglement in chains. Universe is interpreted to mean; many things united as one, and there is no way we can stop being part of it while on earth. Without this unconditional design of nature, we would have been in a "multiverse" with the freedom to choose which of the "verses" to live. But as it is, the universe is believed to be one, and we are conditioned to live in it. This makes the universe a natural chain imposed on all beings living on earth.

Apart from this universal chain placed on us, there are other chains that are natural to man. One of such natural chains is the law. If we want to be free from chains here on earth; then we must do away with the laws. But how can we stay without some laws? This is another burden that is difficult to overcome. Asides the universe, law is the greatest chain to man.

This law is divided into two. The natural law and the one made by man. Natural law is not an enemy to man; it is to guide us to achieve our goals in life. The man-made law is the one we must be skeptical about, because of the egoistic nature of man. Any time a law is made by man, it is always meant to favor some people to the detriment of some. No law maker will ordinarily make a law that will affect his desire. His personal interest is always considered before the rest. That makes man-made law one of the worst chains to man. Right from the ancient days, the laws made by men were seen as legal weapons to protect those in power and not necessarily the weak. This might have prompted Thrasymachus to say that "might is right".

Justice to him is nothing more than the opinion of those in power; it amounts to injustice initiated by the powerful against the weak. This is a form of chain introduced by man against a fellow human being. The more the wrongful chains constructed by man, the more the limitations on the extent he can grow.

We need not worry about the natural chain that nature has bestowed on us. It is those man-made chains that are selfishly constructed that we must fight against. Those in political power are the key actors that are constructing the chains that kill our dreams. Some policies are selfishly put in place, so that the majority of people will suffer, while a few others in power will have it easy. This kind of chain is not natural; they are made by those who do not want others to grow.

Kitoto state is a typical example of this. The primary function of a state is to protect the lives and properties of its members. Another one is to ensure that the social amenities are provided to all, but Kitoto state is not like that. People are killed in their numbers on a daily basis. Life is no longer sacred as they used to say. Something urgently enough must be done; else the people of Kitoto will continue to die in chains that were not naturally meant for them. Apart from the chains the Kitoto government has brought to its people, especially from those leaders that are very corrupt, many occupations are forms of chain, mostly in private business owned by a director who is mean. Staff of such establishments find it difficult to utilize their talents. The chain in private sectors has the potential to kill the staff's desire to work. Some directors of organizations are mean. They do not consider the welfare of their staff. They know that Kitoto's system is corrupt, that is why they treat their staff as they wish. This attitude does not also allow the staff to put in their best. In the end, the overall development of Kitoto is affected.

When a chain becomes so heavy to bear, the struggle to unbind from it becomes a trend. The laws will be broken and the norms ignored, because no one can be comfortable if he is pressed down by a chain. Though it is agreed that being in the chain is natural to man, it should not be the one caused by men.

Many of the chains limiting them from achieving their goals are not natural. They are chains constructed by their leaders to control Kitoto's resources because of greed. Something needs to be done if Kitoto is to be saved.

1

The Kitoto State

Kitoto is a blessed state that is endowed with both natural and human resources. It is highly populated with great and promising people of talents. Though Kitoto is amongst the states the wider society considers underdeveloped, it has produced some individuals whose wealth can feed some states in the developed world. Many of those who make the list of the wealthy class in Kitoto are the ones controlling the pipe that drills the collective natural resources and other wealth of the good people of Kitoto for their personal benefits. Right from when Kitoto had her independence over six decades ago; Kitoto has not grown beyond the experimental level of a people aspiring to be in charge of her self-determination.

Sadly, Kitoto is still indirectly controlled by those who gave her the name "Kitoto". These people do not mean well for Kitoto. Their aim is to use Kitoto to achieve their goal. That is why their eyes are on Kitoto's resources. This selfish intent is no longer strange, many people in Kitoto are aware of it. The main problem now is with some of the Kitoto's leaders, who have refused to take the responsibility to develop Kitoto for the betterment of all, but rather connive with the "Golden Vultures" to ruin Kitoto. The important thing Kitoto people should know is this; there is no one that will volunteer to help you without having his interest to protect. When someone come to render help, try to know what his interest is, to know if you would be able to accommodate, failing to do so, you may live to regret what he will get in return.

Kitoto state has many borrowed and imposed administrative policies that are not functional in addressing the problems facing the people. Many of these policies are from those who officiated the illegal marriage that brought peoples of different cultures and backgrounds together without minding their fundamental differences and peculiarities. These aliens, known as "Golden Vultures," have also imposed their own traditions and cultures on the indigenous people of Kitoto, making them almost lose their true identity as a people. A people's culture is a mark of identity that must be cherished. Shying away from it amounts to self-hate. If the people of Kitoto must regain their uniqueness; they must go back to the culture that defined them as a people. This is one of the things they must not compromise, because every good child must know his root. Anyone who opposes everything about you does not mean well to you. A good person will encourage and appreciate you for what you have, and advise you on how you can correct the wrongs. But when you see someone who condemns everything that is precious to you, know that his intention is not to build but to destroy your roots.

One thing the Kitoto people must note is that; civilization is not about abandoning one's culture. It is to rebrand it and make it better than ever, and not to take another person's culture and make your own. This is a contemporary trend in Kitoto that should be stopped. Adopting a person's culture is an introduction of a new chain in the land. This kind of chain should be avoided. If not, what kind of history will the people of Kitoto tell their children? That their culture is no more to be remembered, when others are busy imposing their own on them? It is said that a fool at forty is a fool forever. Kitoto had reached the age to be wise. They should never again allow a foreigner to destroy their pride. If they do, history will not be kind to them.

Another fundamental thing about Kitoto that is now debased is the laws designed by some leaders past to ensure that they hold onto the staff of authority of Kitoto as long as they live. Such laws only guarantee the safety of those in favorable leadership positions and then become tools of victimization to others already in various kinds of chain. Their operational constitution has not given the people the desired administrative system to make Kitoto a thriving state. They always say that the constitution is superior to an individual, but the power that the constitution is giving to their leader, seems to make the leader superior to the nation; making few individuals to be indirectly powerful and superior to the constitution. Is it not their leader that single-handedly appoints the chief judge of the nation? Even the chief security of the state is appointed at his instance. Soldiers are under his supervision. What then is controlling the leader? If a constitution of a state gives so much power to an individual instead of giving to the people, then that individual has automatically become the law. The sad thing is that those who are supposed to correct this abnormally are not taking it as something that is important. All their concern is to have a sub-head that can give them opportunities to loot. Every other thing is none of their business. This is the present situation in Kitoto state.

The tricks of the "Golden Vultures"

Granted, Kitoto is generally agreed as a sovereign state by the people, but that is only on paper and not in practice. A thorough investigation will reveal that Kitoto is under the control of the "Golden Vultures." These were people who came to Kitoto's land early enough in the pretext of assisting the Kitoto people in realizing their authentic selves. In contrast, their primary intention was to loot Kitoto of her natural and human resources. This pretext was successfully implemented by using the natural leaders of Kitoto to preach against the Kitoto's traditions, worship, and cultures.

They used all the tricks to get their way into the state and established their factories in the name of religion. They introduced a form of education that will make

Kitoto people good memorizers, and not the kind that will make them think with logic, else, they'll discover their tricks and fight for their emancipation. This kind of education can only make them good administrators and experienced managers; so that they will be able to manage the factories of their masters. That is why the aspects of production, invention, and discovery are not in their curriculum. If Kitoto wants to grow as a state, they must redesign their curriculum to include production. Invention and discovery must be taken as projects that must be accomplished, if not, the state will not be free from the foreign chain imposed on the nation.

Even before the coming of the "Golden Vultures," Kitoto had had a system of education which was typically centered on the production, invention, and discovery. But they were tricked to abandon them claiming they were satanic, devilish, and barbaric. The Kitoto people were good at arts work. Sculptor, drawing, and other craftworks were part of their nature. These were amongst the things that made the Kitoto people unique as a people.

The "Golden Vultures" refused to appreciate this diversity of Kitoto's cultures, languages, traditions, ethnicities, and occupations, because they wanted to ensure their plan is executed; the plan to destroy the cultures that made Kitoto people united. They intentionally introduced their own approach to unity that has not really made the people to be united. That was how the idea of the so called united Kitoto came into discussion. It is the unity that brings different corrupt leaders together to loot the people. This does not have anything to do with the development of the nation.

Even some of the indigenes of Kitoto who were exposed enough to defend the rich heritage of Kitoto, were lured through political and religious sentiments to accept the "undefined marriage" that was officiated by the representative of the "Golden Vultures". This forced marriage remains a burden on the head of all sons and daughters of Kitoto. No wonder the agitation for separation by many freedom and justice seekers in Kitoto becomes a paradigm in present times. Many of the Kitoto people are willing to be free from the chain imposed on them by the "Golden Vultures," but the problem is the leaders who are benefiting from the system.

Upon the arrival of the "Golden Vultures" in Kitoto's land, they seized the opportunity of the era of the

Kitotos' ignorance of the value of their rich culture and destroyed their gods. They stole and carted away other sacred artifacts that were original to the Kitotos. And forced them to hate anything natural and authentic to their land; bringing a foreign chain to add to the ones that were traditional to them. If those artifacts were demonic as they claimed them to be, why didn't they destroy them, but they took them to their land? They made the Kitoto people hate their artifacts in their land only to go to the foreign land and pay money to watch them in the museum. When shall the Kitoto people realize that they were tricked? That those they are looking up to are the ones that are supposed to look up to them? Kitotos should know that they have what it takes to make them powerful as a state. The Kitoto people must rise to the task of regaining their heritage. If they do, their land will become the most desired place to be. Why should one have a drum, but play music with his stomach? How pleasant is it to hear that someone is leaving a full cow in his house to his neighbor's to struggle for a half leg of a goat?

In a move to deceive the Kitotos to believe that their God was weak, vulnerable, and incapable of providing for them, the "Golden Vultures" introduced the same

Supreme Being the Kitotos have been worshiping in a color that resembles their own, and told Kitoto people to believe that Satan is black. This calculated attempt to devalue the great tradition and belief system that kept Kitoto together depicts the evil intent some of these aliens had toward the people of Kitoto. That was how they introduced racism, using the image of God as a panacea. This is a mother of anything that could be regarded as corruption. They made it look as if Supreme God was many, and that the Kitotos' own is inferior. Whereas there was no time the Kitotos did not believe in the existence of gods and in one Supreme God.

Before the arrival of the "Golden vultures", the natural leaders of Kitoto always begin their prayers with the saying "God of heaven and gods of the earth" indicating that, though there are many gods, it is only one that is superior to all. So the concept of Supreme Being was not new to the Kitotos as the "Golden Vultures" wanted them to believe. If people should tell others about the gods, Kitoto people are in a better position to lead the way. Kitoto is a state full of gods. Why then should people think Kitoto is ignorant of the gods and how they can be appeased? Why are the "Golden Vultures" so keen about defending the gods as if God is not God enough to defend Himself? Trying to devalue God in one culture and value in another is an affront to the nature of God, because God is the same regardless of the tribe.

The influence of the "Golden Vultures" in Kitoto

The same false impression planted the seed of the inferiority complex in the land, making the Kitotos think that the "Golden Vultures" are better than them. This misconception is still hunting the Kitotos till today. No wonder the leaders of Kitoto are so much dependent on the approval from the "Golden Vultures" before they could act; even on matters that are purely and entirely their own. Kitoto people will remain in the foreign chain until they realize that they are actually in a chain. The chain they have willingly decided to accept. Many leaders of Kitoto have unknowingly enslaved themselves in their land, yet, parading the world claiming to be the deciders of the fate of Kitoto state, without knowing that their attitude of dependency has made them the means for the "Golden Vultures" to get to their ends. This is amongst the things the Kitoto people must know. They must fight seriously to free themselves.

The damages caused by the "Golden Vultures" have added to the self-inflicted wounds the successive leaderships of Kitoto have brought upon themselves. This makes the present state of affairs in Kitoto look as if Kitoto is beyond redemption. The corruption, injustice, social vices, and other ugly sights experienced in Kitoto, are fundamentally caused by the indigenes of Kitoto who are leaders, especially from those of whom the people of Kitoto collectively elected to manage the affairs of the state. The leadership of Kitoto does not have the interest of the Kitoto people at heart. All they are after is their stomach, every other thing is less important.

2

Kitoto's Administrative Style

K itoto, as a state, has conducted series of elections to choose people that could manage its affairs. It is sad to say that even at that, Kitoto has not been that lucky to have good administrators right from when it started bearing the name, Kitoto. Apart from the very few leaders who, in the early period of Kitoto tried to make Kitoto achieve its heights, the successive leaders were acting as if they were drunk. Another set of leaders who could have made Kitoto rise up to their pledge was the one that was not favored by nature with good health and long life. The next is the one who was surrounded by black goats during his reign.

The one with poor health was the only leader who sincerely attempted to bridge all the imaginary and illusionary barriers some bigots in Kitoto created in the name of religion, political affiliation, and ethnic differences. His dream was to treat all Kitoto people in the sense of being sons and daughters of Kitoto first and foremost. Alas! This was the same person that nature did not favor with good health and long life. He died in leading the Kitoto people to cross the wilderness of their limitations. That is why people keep asking why good people hardly last. Is it that nature is not fair to the people of Kitoto by not allowing the righteous to stay long and heal the land? Or, are Kitoto's sins unforgivable? These are amongst the questions people in man-made chains in Kitoto continue to ask. They keep asking because of frustration. The frustration brought to them by their leaders.

His successor had somewhat adopted his philosophy of complementarity as he took over the mantle of leadership of Kitoto. He was determined to tread the path of his predecessor in body and soul, but the people of Kitoto are not fit for a leader that is weak. The predecessor was judged as weak; irrespective of this, he was a man of intense passion and desire to cross this unfriendly wilderness of Kitoto's limitations. His weakness made the way for some of his cabinet members who were so beautiful and brilliant, yet acted like goats. These beautiful and intelligent goats were out to eat all the yams in the Kitoto reserve, while others among them were those determined to see that the good dreams of these unfavorable leaders do not come to reality so long they were on the throne. Thus, they exhibited attitudes that can pave a way for a takeover to quench their dreams. All this accounted for why the efforts of the successor to lead the people of Kitoto to the expected destination were thwarted. This attitude of some of his cabinets contradicted the true identity of his name. The once lucky fellow became so unlucky in his administration, though this may not be the limit to the definitions of his nature.

Apart from these few leaders narrated above, others were primarily dogs who delighted in eating their vomit. These leaders did and are still doing what they stood against while seeking the mandate to lead Kitoto. Others were and are still surrounded by the drilling machines that drill the resources of the Kitoto and store in the foreign land, thus, contributing to the development of the already developed states while at the same time leaving their state in a deteriorating condition. This is not smartness, but stupidity at its extreme. If Kitoto must be great, the Kitotos money must be spent in Kitoto. But who will make the policy, when they are the very people perpetuating the evil act? The Kitoto people should stop their leaders from having industries outside Kitoto, unless they have already established enough of that in Kitoto's land. It is unethical to get money from city A to develop city B, when the said city A is underdeveloped. Before you think of painting somebody's house, ensure that you have built your own. You cannot claim to be a rich man when your family and community people are poor. A truly rich person is not judged by the amount of money he has in the bank, but by the number of his people that have benefitted from his wealth.

Today, the Kitoto people are suffering and are living in great pain and fear. This is on account of bad administrations and the negative impacts of the activities of those who no longer feel comfortable remaining in various kinds of man-made chains. Suffering in several types of chains is typical of anyone who lives in Kitoto as his home. In Kitoto, you must suffer to get anything that is supposed to be freely given to you, even the ones that are naturally your own. Kitoto leaders specialize in giving to others what their citizens are desperately in need of. Their raw materials are only good at development of other states while Kitoto remain in ruin.

When Buddha talked about the four noble truths, he was talking about suffering that comes from the way humans crave for material things that cannot give the much needed satisfaction. He didn't refer to the ones that are introduced by bad administration. The four noble truths of Buddha are: 1. Life is full of suffering 2. The cause of suffering is our craving, desire, or attachment 3. To stop suffering is to stop desiring 4. To stop desiring is to follow the eightfold path. These eightfold paths are the eight rights man is expected to adopt to be free from suffering or some of his chains. They are: Right Understanding, Right Thought, Right Speech, Right Action, Right Livelihood, Right Effort, Right Mindfulness, and Right Concentration. The leaders of Kitoto ought to follow these eight rights if they desire to lessen the chains of their people.

The natural flavor and good taste of Kitoto which they hitherto enjoyed before her independence are diminishing by the day. In recent times, there is no day without a story of those who struggle to unchain themselves from different kinds of leaders-imposed chains taking the lives of those in the chain with them. The leaders of Kitoto have successfully turned the youths of Kitoto against themselves. Even with this, what is uncommon in Kitoto is to see those trying to unbind themselves from chains having access to terrorize or kill those in the "Golden chain". Those in the golden chain are the leaders and the highly placed political class in Kitoto. They have tactically made themselves the lords and gods of Kitoto state. They are now untouchable in the land of Kitoto. They are those who determine the fate of the continuity or the end of Kitoto as a sovereign state, although their plans can only be validated if the "Golden Vultures" have been briefed. This is another indication that even the leaders are also in chains.

But is this class of people really in the chains? Yes! They are. Since it is incumbent on them to protect the interests of all sons and daughters of Kitoto they vouched to protect, their refusal to carry out these constitutional mandates becomes a moral chain they placed upon themselves. Again, their much dependence on the "Golden Vultures" before they could act is an indication of their bondage. This chain will hunt them even when they die. The chain is "Golden" because they have access to the material wealth of Kitoto, which others do not. It is a chain many people desire to have, regardless of the moral burden it will incur for them. Though not all of them are bad, they are few whose paths are straight. These ones always suffer for standing for the truth, and their voices are hardly heard from the crowd. Such leaders, if they succeed in their first tenure, they cannot get the second, because Kitoto political system does not want people who are sincere. That is how their political system is designed; they make it to suit those who are corrupt. Little wonder the holiest among the religious will change when they mingle with them.

The administration of Kitoto does not only need a change of leadership, but a change of the system. The only reason to change a leader is to look for such a leader that will work toward the change of the system. Asides that, no leader can perform when the system is already corrupt. The political system of Kitoto needs a total reformation; else, the people will keep toiling in vain. In every successful state, it is the well-structured system that guides their leaders. And a bad leader can be corrected by a well-designed system set for the nation. Kitoto policies do not give room to make Kitoto to grow, and to compete with other states of the world.

Their educational system is poorly structured. They dwell more on theory without practicality. They are yet to have a template of education that can make them self-reliant. This is too bad for any state in the contemporary world.

Politics with the traditional throne

Another pathetic thing in Kitoto is how the traditional leaders have been reduced to the level of becoming enslaved by those in the political wing. Hitherto, those that were traditionally honored by the gods were the custodians of the ethical codes of Kitoto. They were guided by the gods and were sincere in their dealings with their subjects. The traditional leaders were the ones that made the political Lords. Politicians always show them respect. Today the narrative in Kitoto has turned the hunter to the hunted. Those with political power now decide who should sit on the traditional stool in Kitoto state. The remaining power is in the hands of the religious leaders and the business tycoons. Tell me how a politician will understand the language of the gods more than the traditional priest whose responsibility is to communicate with the gods? How will any of them know the names of the gods and what the gods desire? Indeed, Kitoto leaders have annoyed the gods. They have introduced in the land traditions that are strange to them. All these contribute to the many chains Kitoto is battling with today. If the Kitoto people want things to take their rightful shape; politicians should allow the traditionalists to handle their affairs. They know how to elect their kings and how to manage those under their rule. If they default, the gods shall rise and fight, without any interference from any man. *It is needless to pray for Judas to die, when it is clear that Judas will surely hang himself.* Let politicians stop to fight for the gods. They should as a matter of importance give the traditionalists a chance in order not to attract another chain from the gods.

The traditional leaders themselves have long been diverted from the primary duty of their call. They no longer acknowledge the sanctity of the throne they sit on. Today, the traditional leaders are feeding the gods with foreign food; while at the same time are busy clothing with foreign clothes and sampling shoes that are not of the land. They are now speaking foreign languages to the gods as if they are strangers to the land. Even when they wear traditional attires, they combine with those they brought from afar. These are part of the things that detest the gods. Why should you make your culture look inferior, yet you claim to be the custodian of the culture of the land? Are they saying that what is in their custody is fake? If so, they should vacate the throne and give space to those who appreciate their roots. You cannot be a master of two religions. So if you are not comfortable with the tradition, you must leave the throne. You should allow core traditionalists to sit on the traditional throne for justice sake. Why is someone who does not have faith in the culture of his people, struggles to be the one to be elected as the traditional leader? This goes to show how much the traditional leaders in Kitoto are confused.

The fact Kitoto people should know is this; there is no religion or culture that is bad in itself. They become bad once the people begin to manipulate the culture or the religion in favor of some people against the others. If something is actually bad in their culture and religion, then it is subject to correction, because there is no one without a culture. And no culture or religion can be adjourned to be perfect. Perfection only lies in the hands of the creator; every other thing is a matter of opinion. So let all humans respect their culture. That is why the traditionalists should be given their respect. But they too, must live up to expectations. Human rituals are not to be tolerated; every life is sacred before the creator. Political leaders must refrain from their action; that is, the action of imposing traditional leaders on the people. They should respect the culture of their fathers. These traditions were there before they were elected into their respective offices; why then are they acting as if they are wiser than their forefathers?

These days, instead of the political leaders consulting the gods for counsel, the traditional leaders request from the politicians what the gods should speak to the people. The traditional leaders have turned the gods to be dependents of politicians. The palaces' stool and staff of authority have become tools used by the traditional leaders to beg for political blessings and favors. That is how bad the traditional leaders in Kitoto state have evolved. Some of them have no idea of the sanctity of the throne. That is why they don't attach importance to it. Why should a traditional leader turn himself to a beggar before a politician? This is not a good experience to be discussed in public.

In ancient times, traditional leaders were designated by nature and approved by the gods, but today, politicians decide who should sit on the throne. Hereditary in leadership had long departed Kitoto traditional stool. "Moneygachy" (the rule by money) has become a paradigm in selecting traditional leaders in Kitoto state. The traditional gods have been sold, and some had fled the shore of Kitoto state. The ones left may have remained because they do not have where to run to. The gods in Kitoto are hungry with no one to care for them. This also is a chain on the necks of families whose responsibility was to care for the gods. Many families in Kitoto are suffering as the result of this. What exactly is to be done to heal the land? That question will be better answered by the gods.

Before the gods could speak, I would like to advise that the traditionalists should go back to their roots, and give to the gods what is due to them. Some of the gods were brought from afar, and some were bought within the land. They were so active in responding to the requests the people made to them, until the "Golden Vultures" came to say that they were false. If you so much believe in what the "Golden Vultures" said; it is not my concern, but the manner at which you destroyed these gods is what you must have to rethink. Many of the abominations committed in the

land today may be as a result of this. That is why
people must be careful in the way they act, especially
with things that concern the gods. If the Kitoto people
had celebrated the gods when they were brought to
their communities or homes, why did they not
celebrate them when they were about to be sent away?
We are not against someone embracing a foreign
religion, but the ones that were earlier invited ought
to be ceremoniously sent away before the new is
adopted. Even a bad leader is celebrated when he is
about to leave his throne, how much more the gods
that were good to the land? Why burning things that
have been of help to you? Remember, the law of
karma is real. God Himself dislikes ingratitude of
men, so why paying the gods with ingratitude instead
of praise? It is not that the Kitoto people should hold
onto their traditional worship by all means if they see
it as obsolete. What we are saying is if the Kitoto
people did not want them again they ought to have
properly send them away, by so doing, they would
have fully disengaged themselves from the gods. Since
this was not the case, many Kitoto people are still in
chain of the abuses done to the gods.

Things are not the way it used to be in the land. So
much infiltration of foreign teachings has offended

the gods. Many traditional priests have abandoned the shrines; some are now in churches and in the mosques. They seem to have lost patronage in the shrine, so they resort to exploring areas that are not typical of them. Those who wish to maintain their names as priests in the shrine are hungry today, because the children of Kitoto are no longer consulting them for atonement for their sins, and they have refused to go to them to solicit a year of a good harvest. Sacred forests have long been destroyed. Forbidden days and places of worship are now things of the past. Holy days are no longer observed. All these can in a way multiply their chains.

No wonder the gods are now eating anything presented to them as food. Now, we do not know if the messages from the gods of Kitoto are genuine. The affiliation of traditional leaders with politicians in Kitoto has caused the people to play politics even with the gods. This also contributes to the low patronage in the shrines. Little wonder that the gods of Kitoto are no longer reliable when they speak. These days the gods seem to talk from both sides of their mouth. The reason for this can also be as a result of hunger experienced by the gods. The fear of being entirely rejected by those still consulting them can as well be a factor, or the fear of being banned by the political lords from operating in the land. These politicians were among those that once depended on the gods for guides. This also explains the dynamics that exist in our world. How the searcher becomes the searched.

Religion ought to be an avenue to love

Another problem facing Kitoto is caused by the misinterpretation of the doctrines of the two religions from two brothers (Ifanam and Akwekam) by their respective members. These are the religions that the "Golden Vultures" and the "Eager Lions" brought to the land. While the two beliefs are not wrong in themselves, the way and manner these religions were brought into Kitoto and how the followers interpret the contents of the two sacred books are problematic. The seeds planted by these religions ought to have produced fruits covered with love, instead of this; they have so far created hatred and fight. This is not what the creator wants of them. But their ignorance has turned things into the way they are. This is also a chain invented by men. Religion should be able to enthrone the reign of peace. But in Kitoto, the experience is not the same. The two religions have caused confusion more than what the traditionalists have caused. And the secret behind this crisis is the plan of politicians to use religious crises for their political biddings. That is why they are extending their influences to the church, mosque, and shrines. They want to put everything under their control. They can only control the people and not God. A day is coming that everyone will account for his act. That day they will know that God is God.

One important thing we must know; is that religions are different routes to God. No matter the route you chose to take. The compass that directs the steps always indicates love and peace. Any violence in religion has its root in politics. Such an act is not from God. Because the God I know is the Lord of peace. It is politics that has corrupted the land. I do not know who the Kitotos will send to their politicians, to tell them how dangerous it is; to play politics to the extent of playing it with God.

Kitoto is in ruin

Kitoto is no longer a land to behold. Many people are running out from it for fear of being attacked by those fighting to get out from different kinds of chains. Even the leaders of Kitoto do not allow their children to school or live in the state, because they know that Kitoto is no longer a safe land for people to live. The leaders and their children have long sought citizenship in Capola, Tinkata, Siketo, and many other states with workable systems. This can never be the solution to their woe. A child who doesn't want his mother to sleep, such a child will not also sleep. Today the wealth of Kitoto is sampled in a foreign land. Mansions, schools, hotels, and factories are built with the proceeds from the Kitoto resources in the lands that are not their own. And you think nature will allow them to go without being visited by the gods!

Instead of doing something to fix their state, they are busy making their children citizens of the lands that are not their own. No one has ever become original by changing his root. They should remember that though they have succeeded in changing their nationality, they will never change their DNA. The Kitoto blood is still flowing in their veins. This blood will make them pay for the evil acts they have done to Kitoto land.

The leaders of Kitoto have succeeded in turning their young ones against themselves. They select some of them and train them for war. They buy rifles and bullets and share to them. In the end, the young ones use these weapons to kill themselves, while their leaders continue looting their collective wealth at will. How I wish their youth were wise. They would not allow themselves to be used. They will demand that in every war the politicians want them to fight; they make their children commanders of the war. Everyone has a chain on his neck; it is unwise to fight to free others when your own is still on your neck. Every fight right now should be channeled to free the Kitotos from their chains, other fights are not necessary for now. You cannot be quick to show sympathy to others when they are injured, but refused to say a word when your people are killed.

If the youths want to be free from their chains, they must begin to love themselves and work as a team. It is time for them to know that cultism is not the best way to go. Engagement in education is a sure path to follow. It is high time the youths know that their tomorrow is today. If they truly want to lead by tomorrow, they must begin from today. The only day we are sure of is today. Tomorrow is an illusion because no man in history has ever entered or seen his tomorrow. The very important day in human life is "today." Every other day is a mirage. So why are people hoping for what they are not sure will come. The youths of Kitoto must be wise. The era of ignorance has passed. Now people's eyes have opened, that of the Kitoto's youths should not be different. They should know that to be loyal is not to behave like a slave. You can be loyal and still say "no" to some wrongs. Why should they send you to kill your fellow youths who are merely protesting bad governance and you go? What kind of spirit is working in you? Some of the chains on your neck, you are the cause. Kitoto's youths should not put all the blame on their elders. The elders' own is even better, because they kill you gradually through their bad admirations. That of the youths is hash.

Things have really gone bad in the land. Many youths cannot go to school for lack of funds. Even those who managed to go have not been employed after graduation. Many of them are roaming the street; looking like slaves in the land that belongs to them. Many of the girls have been forced into prostitution, while the boys have resorted to join all sorts of bad gangs. All these are means to survive. But do they really deserve this in the land they have as a right?

The day the youths of Kitoto will rise to fight, Kitoto's state will not contain the wrath.

Kitoto has become a farmland to some of its leaders. They visit Kitoto as someone going to farm for harvest. After the harvest they leave the farm for others to continue to work. A day is coming, when moon will be shining in the morning, there, the secret acts of men would be unfolded. The stolen treasures of Kitoto would be refunded.

3

The Teaching Profession in Kitoto is a Noble Chain

It is not everyone that can teach. Some people see it as a gift, while others say it is a skill; a skill that can only be acquired by learning. Teaching needs patience and time. A teacher must constantly do research to update himself. That is why teachers ought to be taken care of so that they can concentrate to do their work with joy, else, it is difficult to get the best from them. This is how it is with teachers all over the world. But the experience in Kitoto is different. The teachers in Kitoto are in chains. Their salaries cannot take care of their feedings, let alone the rent and other essential bills for an average living.

Almost every worker in Kitoto is suffering; both in the private and public sectors, but the one in the teaching profession is an embarrassment to the state. The teaching profession in Kitoto State is amongst the occupations that have suffered from poor remuneration and general welfare of their workers. Whether in the primary, secondary, or tertiary, the experience is almost the same. This makes many scholars decline the offer to teach, including those who have the needed skills and ability. Apart from the few individuals who have the passion for teaching, others who ventured into education as a profession only accept to do so because of their inability to secure a more lucrative job suitable for them to make a living. Teaching in its ideal status is a noble profession. Still, the government of Kitoto has made it appears that teaching is an endorsement to be in a noble chain; a chain of financial limitations. Kitoto state could have comfortably avoided these chains but they make it look like teaching as a profession is synonymous with suffering or as if it is a curse. How can someone work for a month, and go home with a salary that cannot take care of him for a week? What kind of arithmetic can we use to justify this? Even Aristotelian's syllogism cannot give an answer. The teaching profession anywhere is a noble profession. It is an occupation that attracts so much respect from the people. And also secures an impressive remuneration to the members.

On the contrary, teaching in Kitoto is amongst the least paid jobs the Kitoto government can ever offer to its people. It is sad to hear that teachers in Kitoto are not anywhere better than ten and eleven spanners that are the most used spanners of all. The way these spanners are used is the same way the teachers of Kitoto are being used, especially when the issue of secular election is in focus. The supposed noble profession has long become a noble chain. In Kitoto, no teacher can sincerely boast of any meaningful growth if left at the mercy of his regular monthly remuneration. The profession that is supposed to make its members noble citizens with good welfare packages to make them live comfortably in a society that is blessed with both natural and human resources has instead turned the noble profession into a noble chain of humiliation. This is one of the things the government of Kitoto should look into for the solution so that teachers can be happy.

But should we blame those who have chosen to teach in Kitoto as a profession? No! Instead, they need to be appreciated. They have indeed taken a noble responsibility. But the underlined truth is that they are in chains by all indications. From time to time, they come out to cry that their salary is unworthy to mention in the public. But the leaders of Kitoto kept promising them that something tangible would be done. Many have died in the course of waiting for the day these tantalized promises would be fulfilled, while others have overstayed their service years; thus, they retired. Successive administrations seem not to have made any significant changes in educational sectors in the state. Many of the schools are without learning facilities. There are some that do not have desks for the students to sit, many teachers are without an office to stay and work. Now tell me how well they can perform? The teachers and the students are not comfortable in school; both parties are suffering, yet the Kitoto government wants them to be quiet without complaint. That is why they keep having strike actions now and then. This has really affected the performances of the students in the pursuit of their careers.

It is difficult for a hungry man to give his best. That is why teachers' performances are less optimized. Which research can be successfully done in an empty stomach? How then should we expect so much from a man whose stomach is empty? When you see some of them collecting some "sorting", they may have been pushed to do so because of hunger. In the world, everything is connected to one another, nothing happens completely in isolation. Success is rooted in hard work, just as failure is the product of laziness. You cannot treat teachers badly and expect them to produce good students. How is it possible for "good" to be a product of "bad"? The measure the Kitoto government is giving to the teachers is the same measurement the students are receiving. If the Kitoto state wants to get the best from its students, it must do well with the teachers. The Kitoto state must always remember, that "a destruction of a part is a destruction of the whole." When the teachers are not taken care of, the students can never get the best from them. If the Kitoto state desires for sellable graduates, they must take care of their teachers. If a society wants its citizens to obey its laws, then it must make sure its people are not without some food. No one remembers any rules when he is hungry. That is why you see members of the noble profession indulging in "sorting." Some teachers are now doing it as if it is normal. Something really needs to be done to salvage the situation.

But is it really Kitoto's system that ruined the teachers or is it the teachers that spoiled the system? The problem is not really from the teachers, but from the system Kitoto is operating. To have a better Kitoto, the educational system must be reformed. The first step to the reformation is the welfare of the teachers; the second is facilities for learning. The greatest mistake the Kitoto government has been making is starting the reformation with the second. How can you give money to a man who is hungry to buy drugs for ulcer when he has no food to quench the ulcer? Common sense should tell us that food is the best treatment to ulcer and not the drugs. No matter how powerful the drug is, food is still the solution. It is after the food that you can think of the drugs. This is the paradox of education funding in Kitoto state. The worse of it is that, even the approval of the second (educational equipment/facilities) is always on the media, if the teachers agitate for the implementation, the government will put the approved equipment and its implementation on paper, without any physical equipment in any of the schools to serve as a prove.

Akana meets Spy

Akana, a teacher with the government of Kitoto who was very hungry and without money for food, was on his way to his friend's house for a meal. The friend's name is Kelima. Kelima is Akana's long-standing friend, though they stay some miles apart from each other. Akana came with a big bag as someone who was about to travel, though the bag was not attractive enough to merit a long journey. The hungry teacher was looking so tired and weak, and could only walk, but slowly. On his way, Akana met Spy, one of their friends. Spy is a journalist working in a private broadcasting company. Spy, in his reportage, has received many meritorious awards from reputable institutions. He was noted for his captivating news headlines, though most times, the headlines do not reflect the contents of the news. That was his tactic to make people go for their newsletters. Upon their meeting, this discussion ensued:

Spy: Akana, where are you going with this big bag?

Akana: My guy, I want to see Kelima. Do you know if he is at home?

Spy: Yeah. I saw him through the window when he returned from Sala Drinking Spot.

Akana: I was only asking if he is at home. I did not ask for the itinerary of his movement; this name is really affecting you! You like monitoring people to report their deeds, whether there is demand for it or not.

Spy: So I did wrong for answering your question? If so, I'm sorry.

Akana: That is not what I meant. You like taking every little thing seriously.

Spy: Yes, I don't take things for granted.

Akana: It's okay, Spy, thank you for the info; I hope he's at home like you said. Let me check on him then.

Spy: No problem Akana, enjoy your stay.

Akana in Kelima's House

Kelima, a brother to the minister of education in Kitoto is working with the Election Cooperation Council (ECC), the institution in charge of the conduct of the elections in Kitoto. Kelima was listening to the news when Akana knocked. Akana is a highly respected fellow in the Akwete community. He is a renowned teacher and a disciplinarian. He is seen as one of the most enlightened, educated, virtuous, hardworking, and promising teachers in the community. However, he is in the cadre of those in

Kitoto whose salary does not differentiate the workers from the beggars. Akana entered Kelima's compound and knock at the door…

Akana: (A knock on the door) Anybody home?

Kelima: Yes! Come in, please. Hey! Akana, is, this you? How are you doing? It has been a while; where have you been all this while? By the way, where are you coming from this late with a big bag; any better for me?

Akana: Too many questions! Kel, please, I don't have the strength to answer all these questions. I don't know when you become a lawyer or have you become like Akpakot, the philosopher?

Kelima: You have come again Akana! Anyways, sorry! But where are you coming from?

Akana: Kel, have you forgotten that this is the end of the term; setting exams, marking the scripts and preparing the results to ensure that the students get their results before going for the holiday have kept me busy all through. I have been in the school since morning trying to mark examination scripts. I have to stop over if you have something for me to eat before I get home. Since morning, nothing has entered my mouth, and I didn't have any money to buy everyday things like bread; I was so hungry and weak. Kel, please give me water first; I'm very thirsty too.

Kelima: Akana, you know where the fridge is. Please go and get water and do yourself a favor by preparing something to eat. The kitchen is open.

Akana: You don't even know how to take care of your visitor (laughs).

Kelima: When I see the visitor, I'll surely take care of him. So you call yourself a visitor? But wait ooo! This one that the sleeve of your shirt is now covering your fingers; I hope all is well?

Akana: All well? Is there any time that anything is ever well in Kitoto?

Kelima: You have come again (laughs). You know how to communicate sad news in a jovial way. Come on, Akana! Why should you starve yourself? The month just ended; have you not been paid? As a teacher, being a member of a noble profession, I believe your take-home is reasonable enough to care for your basic needs? I am not complaining that you must eat in my house; the point is that, while sacrificing your time, energy, wealth of knowledge, and resources to give your best to teach, you must spend part of your income to take care of yourself. Guy! Life is one, so enjoy it.

Akana: My brother how I wish the money is there for me to enjoy, but as it is, I don't even have money for my basic needs; Kel, you will not understand. What the teachers of this state are passing through is more than what the mouth can speak. There is nothing to enjoy my brother.

Kelima: Sincerely, I don't understand you, and I wish to. Are teachers having problem with the government or do you lose some members to anything?

Akana: Are you not aware that teachers have not been paid for five months now? Kel, let me inform you for free that I have been in one level for over seven years without promotion, and when I was finally promoted three years ago, I am still collecting my old salary as I speak? Aside from the non-payment, do you ask me what my salary in a month is? I collect 200 tintua in a month, about $70. Kel, tell me how I can survive with this? You see this shirt I'm wearing? A small boy asked me yesterday if my school has a teacher's uniform. I did not understand why he asked the question; when I asked him why, he told me because he always sees me in this one shirt every day. Kel, I was ashamed of myself; I could not give the innocent boy any better response than shouting at him to go away. Right inside me I was crying. I regretted the day I applied for the job. What is the difference between a beggar in the street and I?

Kelima: Honestly, I do not understand you. Are you sure of all that you are telling me now? Are you saying your salary in a month is 200 tintua and that you have not been paid this token for five months now? Please let me understand something here!

Akana: But that is the truth! Have I ever lied to you before?

Kelima: I find it difficult to believe this. Anyways, I will make some calls on this matter because I cannot comprehend what you just said.

Akana: You are very free to do your findings. The way teachers in Kitoto are suffering is what I cannot understand. We are the ones training these so-called leaders. During times for elections, it is us they use. My brother, nothing is ever well in Kitoto, so never ask me again if all is well.

Kelima: To be candid, all is not well in Kitoto. Just before you came in, I was reading on the news the killing of 15 Kitoto's soldiers by the Isoti group this morning and 23 people of Akweti slaughtered in their farms by the Isato sect. Was it not last week that the same Isoti group kidnapped some travellers along Etonko expressway? So asking if all is well in Kitoto is actually one of the absurd questions to be asked in the present state of Kitoto.

Akana: So when I told you I'm hungry, you should know that it has gotten to "I can't help" condition, which is why I came. Maybe you didn't believe or understand me.

Kelima: Akana, I am short of words; I'm just so surprised at all these things you are saying. In fact, I have to call my uncle, the minister, right away. Is it that the ministry of education is no longer in-charge or responsible for what is going on in schools? My uncle, that I know, could not ordinarily want the staff working under his supervision to suffer. Or has he suddenly changed after joining politics? My brother, in this Kitoto, the more you look, the less you see. But I must ask him if he is actually aware of this. I pray his case should not be like the experience we usually have in our department. When the leaders in the leading political parties or what they called "the power that be" will force us to write elections results in their favor, without minding the ethics that guides us as an institution. Yet our big men will command us as slaves filed to match to farm to perfect their deals. My brother we are just sitting on a timed bomb in this state.

The minister of education is another bright, sharp, and intelligent man whose lifestyle reflects a person's attitude to be considered moral. Before his appointment, he was a teacher and a preacher in his religious group. He has always been considered by the people as one of the leading lights that can change the narrative of Kitoto for the better. His appointment into Kitoto's government had raised hope among teachers that many of the issues bothering them would be solved.

Kelima dialed the minister's number, it rang, but the minister did not respond to the call. He tried three times again but to no avail.

Kalmia: He is not picking. But don't worry; I will indeed discuss this with him.

Akana: Hmm! My brother, I'm tired of the whole thing. In fact, I have lost hope of everything about

Kitoto. They keep promising us that something would be done about our salary, till today there is no sign that something will happen. I really appreciate your concern and, most importantly, the food. Do you know you have saved a life!

Kelima: What are friends for? We must be there for each other, and I know you will do even more for me if you are in the position to do so.

Akana: I'm most grateful, my brother. It is time to go. I hope to hear from you when you call him.

Kelima: No problem about that. Do have a great evening.

Akana: and you too!

Not too long after Akana left, the minister returned the call. Kelima told the minister every detail of his discussion with Akana. Although the minister claimed he was not aware of Akana's claim of non-payment of salary. As for the poor remuneration of teachers in Kitoto, he was silent about it. This made Kelima to assume that the minister was not completely ignorant of the sufferings of teachers in Kitoto. Apart from those who tread the path of politics, the few who work in the natural oil farm, and very few others who work where the leaders' interests are well protected, every other worker in Kitoto is in different "respected chains". The chains are respected because they are workers, while many other graduates in Kitoto are roaming the streets. Minister ended the call with the promise to make some findings and call back.

For some years now, the teachers have been embarking on strike on regular bases. Sometimes for weeks, months, and even for a year in extreme cases. The sad experience is that the decision of the government of Kitoto always stands because of the attitude of most leaders of the union. The successive leadership of the Teachers Union in Kitoto always ends up compromising during time for negotiation with the government. The union leaders have consistently betrayed the union. This has caused disunity among them especially when a crucial decision is to be taken. The Kitoto government is taking advantage of this disunity to get its way anytime the government goes into negotiation with the teachers. Many leaders have been dispossessed of their positions because of this.

It was not too long before the union elected another executive body. The new leadership had promised to lead the union to achieve its main goal, which was, welfare of all the teachers. The leadership did not waste time to send a communiqué to the Kitoto government, demanding an audience of the president through the Education Minister. After three months of waiting without a reply, the teacher's union leader summoned a meeting for the members to agree on a strike action if the government of Kitoto fails to attend to their demands. Spy, the journalist knew what the teachers and their leaders were up to, so he made his way to the venue of the meeting.

4

Meeting of the Association of Kitoto's Teachers

The meeting witnessed teachers from different institutions. There were not too many smiles on their faces. Some of them were like people who have been fasting for a week or more, while others were like people returning from bush clearing in a farm.

Union leader: Great teachers of Kitoto!

All teachers: Great!

Union leader: Great nation builders!

All teachers: Great!

Union leader: I call you all today for this very crucial and essential meeting that will make us see the need to stand as a union with one voice. We are here to resolve and draw the attention of the government of Kitoto to the severe maltreatment this government has brought on us. We must officially and appropriately inform the government that we are no more comfortable with the manner we have been treated. For about three months now since this noble union sent a letter to the government of Kitoto seeking an audience so that we can table our problems before the government. As of this moment, there is no response from them to that effect. I have sent more than three reminders as a fellow up, but to no avail. This is not how teachers should be treated.

I have been privileged to visit more than five states outside Kitoto, and I have seen how their teachers are treated. None of our highly-paid teachers can be compared to the least paid staff in those places I have visited. But here we are, working as an elephant but eating like an ant in a state that is highly blessed with abundant natural resources. None of them can deny that we work tirelessly to ensure that the children of Kitoto are given sound education. Education, they say, is the life wire of every nation. If the leadership of Kitoto really believe that education is truly the life wire of a country, they ought to have done well to understand that teachers are the transmitter of the current into this wire. How will there be a free flow of life in the wire if the transmitter is bad?

All teachers: That is the question (they chorused).

Union leader: Are we not the ones that trained many of the so-called political leaders of Kitoto that are now behaving like Deputy God? Can any of the teachers who have worked for 35 years boast of 5% of what they have acquired in just four years or less? How much is our salary and how much is theirs? Are you aware that what some political leaders go home with in a month is more than some teachers' salary for 35 years put together? We toil and try to write lesson notes. We ensure we cover our syllabus in every academic year. Are we not the same people who taught them and their children? We are the very people who protected them and corrected them anytime they went astray. Some did not merit graduation, but as mothers and fathers, uncles and aunties who wish their children nothing less than success, we made extra classes to ensure that even the dullest among them passed. Our prayer had always been that, when it is well with them, it would be well with the people of Kitoto, including us. Are the gods no longer answering prayers of men? Yes! It is well with political leadership, but why is it not well with the rest of us who nurtured them to become who they are today? This is why I called on all of you today to remind us that being silent in the face of these wrongs is a sin. I firmly believe that God is going to fight for us.

Asandia: Sir, you have spoken well, but my fear is this attitude of always wanting God to do everything for us. I pray that day won't come when some of us will finish defecating and then call on God to assist to clean our anus. I am conscious that most of you are pastors and imams; you will always want us to hand over everything to God. Handing over everything to God is a display of cowardice and laziness. Can someone tell me why God gave us the sense of reasoning? Was it for us to use it to hand over everything to Him to do for us, or to use it and solve some of our existential problems? The earlier we understand that God will never do what He had already given us the power to do for ourselves, the better for us.

Most of you are familiar with the story of Jesus raising Lazarus from the dead as recorded in John 11:38-44. When Jesus got to the tomb, he did not start with prayer. The giant stone that was covering the tomb needed to be removed first. Removing the stone is something that people who need Lazarus back to life should do. Therefore, they were to do that before God could act. God requires our commitment for Him to work for us. He needs us to do those things within our reach before He can act.

Jesus wanted them to play their own part, which was possible for them and then allowed God to do the impossibility. Prayer is never an answer to a problem that can be solved humanly without much stress. The big stone covering the tomb of our stagnation is the bad leaders. It is left for us to plan on how to remove the stone, if the stone is there to stop our progress and deny us our due. The giant stone is the bad leaders in Kitoto state. Until we resolve to remove them, our prayers will all be in vain.

The sad thing is that when the opportunity comes for us to remove the stone through the election, we will be the very people that will sit on the stone and press down on the tomb instead of removing it. How will God answer our prayers when He has given us power to roll out the stone covering our progress?

This is a physical battle, so it needs a physical fight. And it is all of us that must rise and fight for our rights.

God will only support us if we are ready to take up the physical war. He will never fight the physical battle with a spiritual weapon. We can only allow spiritual warfare for God, but for the physical war, we must fight. Greatest Kitoto teachers!

All teachers: Great!

Asandia: I rest my case!

Union leader: You have made a point, as I said earlier on, that my call on all of you was for us to strategize how we can take our destiny by our own hands. With your reaction, I am sure we shall achieve our goal.

Akana: Sir, you have spoken well. Teachers in Kitoto have become laughing stocks. We are being threatened by our landlords and landladies with quit notice, because of our inability to pay our house rent when the time is due. How will we pay on time when the government of Kitoto has not paid us when the time is due! Most of our children cannot go to school anymore because of the school fees increase. They increase the school fees in the schools we teach, but they don't increase our salary, what a paradox! How nice is it to drive my child away from school because of fees, and I am there in the same school to teach their children?

Some of us cannot change clothes again, except for the ladies whose sources of income are not so clear.

A lady teacher (Dora): Akana, what is all this? We are here trying to solve our collective problem, and you are there talking about something else. We are all teachers and our source of income is salary.

Akana: Good question! No doubt, we are all teachers, but the way our ladies appear in costly dresses remains a miracle to some of us. Yes! We are all teachers, but why is the condition of us men like this (Akana threw his hands open and ran his eyes all over his body)?

Dora: Is this a kind of envy or what? Misogyny?

Akana: Who am I to envy her royal majesty?

Union leader: That is okay! Akana and Dora that should be enough; let this not divert our attention from the crucial issue that brought us here.

Head teacher: Exactly!

Union leader: Now, what is your opinion concerning the issue I presented before you?

Head teacher: To me, we should send a delegation to the minister of education to make our demands known since they have refused to honor our letter. If they refuse to oblige this time, we shall not have any other option than to embark on an indefinite strike; enough is enough!

Akana: Thank you, my boss, you have spoken our minds. I have been looking forward to seeing a day like this. Yesterday I was with one of the minister's relatives; I told him all that teachers are passing through in this state. He was shocked. I was surprised to see him pick up his mobile phone and dial the minister's phone number right before me. Unfortunately, the minister did not respond to his calls till I left. But he promised to let him know what we are passing through; who knows if he would be of any help to us. All these politicians, especially here in Kitoto, are not to be trusted.

Union leader: Thanks, Akana; whether he will respond positively to it or not, we have decided to take our destiny into our hands. I'm happy that at least you have sent the message across to him; it would echo to his heart that all is not well with the teachers of Kitoto. Thanks so much for your effort.

Dora: I support what the head teacher has said. We should send a delegation to the government through the ministry of education.

Union leader: Yes, Head teacher and Dora; that is a good one! Then what are our demands?

Susa: When meeting with them we should demand: an increment of salary, study grant, good welfare package, and good pension scheme for all teachers. I hope I have spoken your mind?

All: You are right! Well-spoken!! That is what we want!!!

Union leader: Is there any other thing to add?

Sparta: The government should provide a good housing scheme and should give each of us a loan for a car.

Union leader: Great teachers, how about that?

All teachers: It makes sense!

Union leader: Alright! The union executive will book an appointment with the minister for a meeting before the end of this month. As the leader of this noble union, I will not relent until our goal is achieved. I promise not to disappoint you. This injustice must end. Why should politicians earn so much but we earn this low? This injustice is too much to bear.

Economic Teacher: My leader, you have spoken well, but my problem is with the attitudes of most of our leaders. We have been betrayed severally by our leaders. It is my earnest prayer that this present leadership should not fail us. It is very embarrassing that some of us here will turn back and betray the union at a little cost. Can't our leader hold their throat for once? Are they the only people with families to take care of? Don't we all have families to run? Why can't our leaders respect themselves for once?

Akana: My brother, you just made a point.

Union leader: My fellow teachers, many of you are witness to what I have passed through in the course of protecting the interest of this noble union. You could recall how I slept in cells, and how my salary was withheld for months all in the name of fighting for the good of the union. Would I now betray the same union? All I need from you is your support. In the end, all of us will have a reason to smile.

Akana: We really like the way you lead the union so far. Who knows whether you are doing this to get your way to the "negotiation table" to get your share? Your predecessors had appeared to be more serious and committed in the issues of the union than you are.

But in the end, they always betray us. Can anybody tell this union of any of the past leaders that did not build mansions and buy exotic cars before the end of his tenure? Where did they get the money to build? If it was their salary, why are we not able to build even a small bungalow for ourselves?

My leader, if you want us to escort you to the negotiation table where the union interests would be jeopardized, we will do. After all that is how we have been helping other leaders to go get their share. But how long shall our leaders be the ones to betray our trust?

Union leader: my comrade, take me by my words. I will prove to you that in Kitoto, there are people who are sincere, and that I am one of them.

After the Union leader's speech members sang solidarity songs and departed with a resolve to work as a family until their demands are made.

After the meeting

All this while, Spy was at the meeting to witness the proceedings. It was not up to 2 hours after the meeting that the deliberation of the meeting started filtering into the public space. Spy, the journalist, did not waste any time in making the news headline of the meeting in a popular national newspaper. It was not up to 12 hours that the minister of information began to give dire warning to teachers through some members in the ministry to stop them from carrying out their planned strike.

On hearing this, the union leader called one of his colleagues who incidentally was one of the directors in the ministry of education, to brief him of the planned action and solicit his guide.

The union leader was informed by the director of the memo sent to the department by the minister of education, warning the ministry's staff to resist any plans of strike action by the teachers' union. This of course was the directive from the office of the president through the information minister. However, the director promised to feed the leader with the necessary information of the minister's plans, and he further promised to give background support to their agitation. He therefore advised him to begin their action with a meeting with the minister and other stakeholders, rather than start with a strike. The union leader was pleased with the idea and promised to do likewise.

Without wasting time, another letter was sent by the Union leader to the minister to that effect; soliciting his audience. The letter's content necessitated the minister to call for an impromptu meeting of all the directors of the ministry to have first-hand information on the factuality of the complaints brought before him by the union before meeting with their leaders. The minister is a thoroughgoing man; he doesn't rush into issues without getting some facts.

5

The Minister Meets with the Directors of the Ministry of Education

The meeting was slated for 11 am on a Wednesday. Every head of the various departments in the ministry was in attendance. Each department was expected to brief the Minister of their activities, especially on the implementations of the teachers' approved proposals and those that are yet to be approved.

At the meeting, after the formal protocols, the minister called on the permanent secretary in the ministry to quickly give a rundown of what he knows about the teachers' agitation and the extent the government have so far responded. After the secretary's briefing, the minister further called on each of the directors to tell the forum the effort made by their departments to ensure quick approval and implementation of the teachers' demands. The directors of different departments took turn to brief the minister circumstantially on each of the issues raised by the union. At the end of their reports, they stated the position of the ministry on each of the issues. Before the meeting, the minister had sent some of his aides to the ministry for a secret investigation. The minister needed to know the true state of affairs in the ministry before his meeting with the Union and the Presidency respectively. From their reports, the ministry held the position that some of the Union's demands have long been approved and implemented except for the few that the government is yet to approve. The report was somewhat different from what the minister's informants submitted after their investigation. It was from the two sources of his information gathering that the minister suspected conniving between some heads in the ministry and few members of the union. The minister inferred from the two contradictory reports and from the document available in his office that few of the listed demands of the union were approved by about 10%

of what the union requested, but that it was about 4% that was implemented. The remaining 6% was alleged to be embezzled by some heads of the ministry and that of the union.

It is sad to know that out of a 100% demand made by the Union to the government, only 10% was approved and the 10% did not get to the union. Some elements in the ministry and some union leaders smiled home with 6%, leaving the entire teachers and the educational facilities with just 4%. While government must be held responsible for this, those elements must not go unpunished. The minister was not happy about the development. He promised to meet with few heads in the ministry for further enquiry. What these few elements in the ministry and union have done is disheartening, but why is the government not taking education of its citizens seriously? The Kitoto government is noted for its style of running into signing agreements with the union, but never has the government fulfilled any of their agreements. Part of the things the approved 10% was meant for was for the payment of some allowances of teachers in various institutions, while the remaining was for research grant. The amount that was available for the research grant could only cover less than 5% of the total number of members who applied for it. Before now, Spy had revealed that the amount approved for the payment of the allowance was not up to the amount applied for. And that the amount shared on this purpose was not up to 50% of the amount released by the government. In Kitoto, no one can tell which of the information is correct; whether that of the government or the union. The journalists are not also to be trusted. That is why a good investigation is difficult to conduct in Kitoto.

The minister recalled how one of the union members narrated his experience during the disbursement of the approved allowance. The member disclosed that even the little that was approved did not pass through the right route to the various institutions it was meant for. Having passed through different streets and roads, some amount from the total sum was said to have been diverted to some offices before it got to the approved destinations. When it finally arrived the respective institutions, those who expected to go home with millions of tintua, were collecting in thousands, while the ones who expected in thousands, were going home with hundreds. How it was calculated remains a mathematical mystery to even a Professor of mathematics. The experts in logical reasoning could not comprehend the logical connotation used by the management for the disbursement. In Kitoto, there is nothing that is not possible. The more you try to understand how things are done in Kitoto, the more you become confused.

In the course of the meeting, it was also revealed that other yet to be granted demands were failures on the part of the government, of which the minister disclosed to the directors his readiness to ensure that the government attain to all the union's demands as it was the government responsibility to take care of the welfare of its workers.

By inference, the minister had admitted that the increment of teachers' salary, welfare, and some other incentives have been neglected by the successive administrations of Kitoto. However, he had maintained that the present leadership is trying their best to make sure the welfare of teachers is improved. At the end of the meeting, the minister urged the directors to always put the ministry's interest first before their personal interest, while informing them of the need for a periodic meeting to appraise the ministry's activities. His meeting with the heads of the ministry was to be communicated to the concern members later.

After the meeting, a letter of invitation was sent to the union, inviting the stakeholders of the union for a meeting with the minister. On receiving the letter, the union leader was happy with the progress and quickly informed other stakeholders. That was the first time the union was to meet with the minister since he resumed as education minister.

6

Meeting of the Union Leaders with the Minister

The meeting of the union leaders and the minister was scheduled for 10am. At about 9:30 am, the leadership of the teachers' union and other members of the ministry of education had already seated for the commencement of the meeting. Spy was seen at the premises going up and down with an office file loaded with documents as someone who is preparing to file a murder case in court. At 10am on the dot, the minister and his entourage alighted from a car and moved straight to the hall with stern looking policemen walking beside him. As he approached the hall entrance, there was a call for order by one of the directors from the ministry; "standstill everywhere!" Everyone stood up while the minister walked to his seat. After sitting, every other person did the same. The minister, without waste of time went straight to the matter of the day by calling on the leader of the teachers' union to make his presentation.

Union leader: Mr Minister I sincerely thank you for the opportunity you granted us to have this august meeting with you. We are indeed grateful. Sir, we are here to make known to you some of the challenges facing the teachers in Kitoto and then solicit your intervention. Sir, I want to assure you that I will be very brief in my presentation, knowing how busy you are. Permit me, therefore, to go straight to the point and present our collective demands for your kind consideration sir! Mr Minister, it will surprise you to hear that for about 5 months now, many teachers have not received their monthly salary; yet, they go to work every day. It sounds good to the ears when the name salary is mentioned, but the question is; how much is the salary of an average teacher in Kitoto? Sir, I want to clarify to this respected forum that here in Kitoto, a level 8 teacher is receiving 200 tintua which is about $70 as salary for a month, yet, you will not see it at the end of the month. Sir, while we frown at any delay in the payment of salary, we unconditionally demand an increment of our salary, study grant for qualified teachers, prompt payment of salary, and other allowances like the ones enjoyed by the politicians of Kitoto. The union also demands a good pension scheme for retired teachers and a workable housing scheme for all teachers.

Mr Minister, Sir, for a long time now, the teachers in Kitoto have been neglected by the successive governments. We are always the least to be considered when the welfare of Kitoto's workers is mentioned. We have written many letters, communiqué, and memos to the ministry of education, Kitoto's law making body, and other personalities in the state, yet nothing tangible has been done.

Sir, let me inform you that some of our children can no longer go to school because of the increment in school fees. How can we justifiably explain to someone that our own children cannot go to school because of school fees? Can anybody tell me why the hunter should become the hunted? Why should the teachers be treated so unjustly?

Sir, you will not believe the kind of challenges most of us are going through before paying our house rent and other utility bills. Mr Minister, it will surprise you to hear that most teachers are operating the 0-1-0 level (eating once a day), and many of us cannot even change our clothes anymore. Just yesterday, a teacher in Okpokos Community High School, where I teach, slumped while teaching, and was rushed to the hospital. Several tests were conducted on him to know the cause so that proper treatment can be administered. Mr Minister, could you believe what the result of the test was? I am saddened to inform you that the results of the various tests did not show any severe ailment apart from an ulcer. The doctors' diagnosis showed clearly that the young man was not eating well, hence he died. Is it not sad that a man of noble profession died of hunger in active service? May his soul rest in peace!

All: (echoes) Amen.

Union leader: Mr Minister, the man (Teacher) in question has four children; the youngest is just a week old. Just imagine what that family is going through right now! What is the provision the Kitoto government has put in place to take care of a situation like this? Why should a government starve to death someone who devotedly sacrificed his services for the betterment of Kitoto? He died without receiving his five months' salary. Had it been the so-called salary was paid as of when due, our dead comrade would have been alive today. How can someone live in the chain, suffer in it, and die in it? A noble profession has become a noble chain, what a paradox! Where have the teachers of Kitoto gone wrong? We are here to be corrected if we have offended the government or the gods of Kitoto.

Sir, thus far, the government of Kitoto has been unfair to us. It is for all this maltreatment that the union resolved to meet with the government through your office to see that this omen of unjust treatment is brought to an end. Thank you, Mr Minister, for giving us the audience to air our grievances. We believe that this meeting will not be like every other one the union has had with the past governments.

Minister: Once again, I thank you for coming. Having listened to your well-elaborated complaints, I confess that it is indeed a sad one. Despite that, I understand that many of you might not know the effort this government is making to ensure that the welfare of its entire staff is well taken care of. Not up to three months ago, the government of Kitoto approved 300 billion tintua for the ministry of education to address some of the long demands of the Union. It will interest you to know that just last week; the ministry had submitted another proposal for salary increment pending the executive council's approval. The government is not relenting in the discharge of its responsibilities, and I want to assure you that very soon, the teachers in Kitoto will be amongst the well-paid citizens of this nation. I will present all your demands to the president in the next executive council meeting. Does any other person have something to say? As your leader has said, this meeting is going to be brief.

Akana: Thank you sir, I am happy to see you face to face today. Some weeks ago I was with your younger brother; Kelima in his house. I went there after a daylong work of marking examination scripts of my students. I was in school throughout that day to ensure that I met the deadline. Sir, could you believe that from the morning of that day to the evening that I left the school, I did not eat even a loaf of bread. I was so hungry to the point that my eyes were turning. I had to walk slowly all the way from Santata Model High School where I teach to Serete Street where your brother lives, just for a meal before I could go home. I didn't have any money on me and there was no food at home too. Going to the house from the school would have been a suicidal journey. I needed to look for where to eat. Being a teacher in Kitoto is a disgrace; I must confess. I told your brother everything and he was shocked. He asked if you are aware of the situation. Sir, I am from Usazo; a nearby community to yours. You are one man people so much believe in. Majority of the people had believed that with you in the ministry, being someone who had passed through this experience before, you will fight for the interest of your former colleagues. As it is, we do not know if our imagination was correct. I was with Kelima when he called your mobile line, unfortunately you were not picking. Sir! Teachers in this state are suffering. Let any of the teachers here say if his/her salary can comfortably take him/her for a week? Sir, if I should tell you that for more than five years now, I have not entered market in the name of buying clothes for myself, you will not believe, but that is the truth. Yet, everyone expects teachers to be neat. Even in this hall now, look at us and look at the team that comes with you. Without a little mistake, a visitor to this gathering can correctly differentiate us the teachers from the rest of you in terms of dressing. Why should it be so? I regret the day I collected appointment letter as a teacher in Kitoto. I have put in twenty (20) good years in this job, yet I am still leaving in a rented one bedroom apartment with my wife and four children. I keep stacking chairs and table in the night to create space for my children to sleep. How can such furniture last? As I speak, I don't know if there is any teacher here that can boast of 300 tintua in his/her account. When shall the teachers stop talking about what to eat and begin to talk about building a house and buying a car? Would it be a curse if a teacher should build a moderate and decent house to live? I take my twenty years in service as a teacher as wasted years of my life. I don't know what kind of miracle will make me recover them. My heart is heavy.

The leader union: Akana it is okay, you have made your point. You know Mr Minister is a busy person, we should allow him to go take care of other issues since we have made our points clear to him.

Atete: This is the kind of thing I don't like. Please, leader, allow teachers to pour out their heart. It is a rare privilege we have to sit with the minister. You should allow people to speak their mind. We should not try to be holier than the Pope. This is not a time to behave like a Saint; we are wounded lions, we are already angered. Let no one try to quench a fire from a furnace with the burping wind from the mouth, it will not work.

Minister: Gentlemen! That is enough. I understand your pains and I want to tell you that I share them. As I have said earlier, I will discuss this in the upcoming Council's meeting. Hopefully, something reasonable would be done. I assure you!

Union leader: Thank you sir for your kind words. The association hopes to hear from you soon, Sir. My respected comrades, I was not in any way trying to stop you from expressing yourselves. I was only saying that Akana has made a good point which I know the minister had taken note of. Why will I stop you from pouring out your mind? You should know me by now. I want to solicit this house to give peace a chance at the moment until we hear from the minister again. Great teachers of Kitoto!

All: Great!

After the meeting, the members gathered in groups to discuss the outcome of the meeting. Spy was found in their midst interviewing some of the participants on their take on the deliberation. It was not more than 3 hours that a private television broadcasting company flashed breaking news with the headline "The Teachers Union leaders compromised their stance while meeting with the minister of education". Spy is noted for giving captivating news headlines to attract readers' attention. His news headlines are always the opposite of the contents.

The said meeting with the minister took place on a Friday, so the Union couldn't address their members immediately after the meeting. On Monday, teachers were found trooping into the road leading to the Union's secretariat. Some union members were already at the gate of the secretariat, while some were holding different kinds of cardboard and inks, others were found writing various inscriptions on placard. Inscriptions like: union leaders tell us the truth! Our leaders have betrayed us! Stop the compromise! The union leader must resign! Teachers are suffering, and many other inscriptions. Apart from those at the gate, other members were sighted inside the secretariat, standing in groups of three, four, five, etc., discussing the alleged compromise by the Union's leadership.

Those at the gate were ready to demonstrate as a warning to their planned strike, while those inside were of the opinion that members should be patient for the leadership to address them before they know their stance.

While this was going on, Spy was sighted interviewing some members of the Union on their take on the purported compromise of their leaders. At exactly 8:15 am, some members of the executive of the Union who attended the meeting with the minister began to enter the premises. The first person to enter the secretariat was the association's PRO, who drove in his "push and start" old 504 Peugeot car; some others came in a commercial bus, while others used taxis. At about 8:20 am, the union leader drove into the secretariat in his 2001 model Toyota Camry with an alarming sound because of the leakage in the exhaust pipe of the car.

Alighting from the car, the leader moved straight to the conference hall, where other members were seated to address the crowd. At the instance of the leader's arrival, members trooped into the hall singing different kinds of solidarity and war songs. The union leader tried to call for calm, but all fell on deaf ears. It

took the intervention of the head teacher of Nkube
High School, Mr Asato, to calm the agitators. And just
when there was some level of calmness, Asato echoed
another war-like solidarity song thus:

<blockquote>

Another challenge ooo,

Another challenge ooo,

Another challenge ooo,

Double double challenges ooo.

</blockquote>

All: Another challenge ooo,

Another challenge ooo,

Another challenge ooo,

Double double challenges ooo.

Asato: Leader challenge ooo,

Minister challenge ooo,

President challenge ooo,

Double double challenge ooo.

All: Another challenge ooo,

Another challenge ooo,

Another challenge ooo,

Double double challenges ooo.

Asato continued to chant while others kept responding. All members responded with the intense zeal of an enkindled spirit of unity. The song lasted for about 10 minutes, while members danced and exchanged pleasantries. In the heat of the song, Asato said:

Asato: Greatest teachers of Kitoto!

All: Great!

Asato: Ever conscious Kitoto teachers!

All: Great!

Asato: My fellow Comrades today is yet another memorable day in the history of this union, a day in which a crucial decision will be reached, a decision that will determine the future of teachers in Kitoto. A toad does not run during the day for nothing. Our gathering today will likely change the narrative of the entire teachers of Kitoto. An adage says you don't kill somebody without allowing him to air his view. I know that some of us are disappointed at the news we heard after the meeting of the leadership of this union with the minister. The information of the alleged compromise by our leaders is really a sad one. But, our leaders are here. We must hear from them else we erroneously jump to conclusions. We should know that "unless opposites are taken into consideration, enquiry is incomplete." We cannot conclude without hearing from those who represented us at the meeting.

Mr Asato is a friend to the union leader; this made some members turn down the request by Asato. It took a lot of effort for the union leadership to calm the situation, as some angered members were already accusing the leaders, including Asato, of betrayal. But in truth, Asato was innocent of the accusation as well as the union leader.

After the uproar that took about 30 minutes, a physics teacher who was among those agitating for the demonstration stood up and called for calm; when the hall experienced some level of calmness, the physics teacher addressed the crowd in this way:

Physics Teacher: Great Kitoto teachers!

All: Great!

Physics Teacher: Greatest articulated teachers!

All: Great!

Physics Teacher: My dear comrades, as we all know, the essence of today's gathering was to get feedback on the message this noble association sent to Kitoto government through our leaders. It is wise we allow them a chance to brief this noble house on the outcome of the meeting. Before now, some of you might have heard on the news that the discussion was not fruitful; that the leadership of this noble union who went to speak on our behalf had compromised the union stance. We do not want to jump to conclusions from unverified source. The people who represented our interests at the meeting are right before us. We are all responsible members of the union; it would be unethical to act by assumption, which is why I called for calm so that the union leader may address us. Our action or inaction will solely depend on our representative's message of the outcome of the meeting. Is that okay by us?

All: True talk! Let him talk well, ooo!! Let him go on!!! (they chorus).

Leader union: Great noble teachers of Kitoto

Some members: Great!

Leader union: Great articulate Kitoto teachers

All: Great!

Union Leader: About three weeks ago, we gathered in this same hall at the instance of my personal effort as the leader of this noble union to discuss issues that bother on the overall welfare of teachers in Kitoto. Our communiqué was explicit, stating all we unanimously agreed on as our challenges. That communiqué became our collective voice and our resolve. You could also recall that I made several attempts to meet with the minister to make our stance known to the government of Kitoto. It was just last Friday that the golden opportunity came. Those who attended the meeting can testify to what I presented. As administrative procedure demands, we did not expect the minister to endorse all our requests right at the meeting. He is not the president of Kitoto. Even if he was the president, he would still need to consult widely before reaching any decision. The minister had assured us that he would present our matter before the president in the possible soonest time.

My wife drew my attention to the purported news' headline-flash on Friday night. Contrary to the misleading headline, the content of the news reads: "the minister has resolved to present the issues brought before him by the teachers' union of Kitoto to the president for consideration". On this note, the union leadership has shielded their sword on their planned strike pending the outcome of the presentation". This morning, I had to look for a newspaper vendor to get a copy of the paper. Here is the newspaper publication with this misleading headline (he handed over the newspaper to one of the teachers).

My fellow comrades, I do not know how many of you have patiently read the contents of this news or you were only carried away by the headline? Please let any comrades tell me where the suspension of our planned demonstration and strike to hear from the president becomes a compromise? I have been telling you that we should not always jump to conclusions without hearing from the parties involved. As the physics teacher, Mr Omusa has rightly said; until opposites are taken into respective recognition, enquiry is incomplete. Making enquiry and thorough findings on matters ought to be a norm for us all.

I will assure you that the present leadership of this noble union will stop at nothing to ensure that not even one of our demands will be left unattended. We have suffered enough! Look at my car out there (he points at his old model Toyota Camry) is that the kind of car I should be driving? I entered this secretariat 5 minutes behind the scheduled time; it was not intentional. I actually came out early enough, but my car battery was giving me a problem. I was supposed to have changed it long ago, but where is the money? It was my neighbor who helped me with his battery. As I was coming, one of my front tyres busted; if not God, I would have been in the hospital by now if not in a mortuary. The tyres have expired since, but I can't change them. You might have heard the sound of the car when I came in; when I leave this place, I am going straight to the mechanic workshop to weld the exhaust. Though I do not have the money right now for it, I just believe God that the man will not mind that I pay him later; he is the one that always work on my car anytime I have the related challenge, so he will likely have patience with me. What I am passing through depicts your daily suffering as teachers in Kitoto. How then will I betray the trust that you collectively vested in me? I know your action is predicated on what the past leadership had been doing.

To tell you the truth, since we began this action, I have received several calls from different quarters demanding for a "behind the scene settlement," but my conscience could not allow me to do anything contrary. Yes! I would have loved to drive a brand new car and build a duplex for myself, but I don't think it would be wise to do so to your detriment. I know what teachers are passing through. As I speak, there is one of the teachers whose wife has packed out from their matrimonial home. She based her reason on lack of food in the house and the constant complaint by the husband that he does not have money to provide for the basic needs of the family. The woman said she cannot endure hunger anymore. The woman accused her husband of squandering his money with friends on drinks. But the question is where is the money?

I personally went with the comrade to the wife's family to beg her to return home, at least for the sake of their three promising kids, but she refused. The children were crying beckoning on their mother to come back home with them. I could recall when one of the kids said; "please mummy don't leave us alone daddy will start having money tomorrow." I was shocked when the mother looked straight into her little daughter's face and told her to go and stay with their father, that she will never go back with them.

The child in question should be about four years old. On hearing the response of the mother, the innocent children wept uncontrollably. Tears came out of my eyes.

The mother in-law did not in anyways help the matter. She was insisting that her daughter does not deserve such a man. This is the same man that graduated with a first class honor in engineering. Imagine what the Kitoto's system has subjected him to? That was when I knew that the working of nature is difficult to understand. If our comrade were to be in a state that values education, the story of his progress would have been that of praises and not of shame. When the young man was asked to speak, he stood for about five minutes without uttering a word. He struggled to speak, but could not, but rather burst into crying. It was sad to see a man that has put in all his best to make Kitoto better and with his meager salary; try to ensure his family is not without food in a day weeping like a child. At this point, the father in-law was touched, and then called him to himself and talk to him as a man. It was not a day any right thinking man can forget; a day that man's sincere effort was rewarded with humiliation.

Sir, before his appointment to teach, the young man was working with a reputable company of which the salary was encouraging. He resigned for two reasons. One was for his passion for teaching, and the other was to secure a pensionable job. Who knows if he will not die before the time?

Now tell me, how can this man survive in this kind of situation? Taking care of the kids and preparing notes of lesson. Will the students not be at the receiving end of this tragedy? The root of this problem is not that of the family, but Kitoto's government. This is just a fraction of what is going on in different homes of those who offered themselves to teach.

Greatest Kitoto teachers! I do not want to go further. Right now my heart is heavy. I will suggest we should allow posterity to judge us.

After saying this, he bowed his head and pressed one of his hands on his chest and stood for a while without a word. Some female teachers started wiping their eyes, while some men bowed their heads.

Physics teacher: Great Kitoto teachers.

All: Great!

Physics teacher: Can we now understand why I always say patience is a virtue? From what the leader has told us, unless those who attended the meeting will stand up to contradict him, I don't see where our able leader has gone wrong or compromised in this matter.

I do not doubt the competency of the present leadership in leading the union in the path of liberation. I will solicit our support rather than criticize them without justification or fact.

After the clarifications, the leader thanked everyone and reassured them of the resolve of the executive to make the union proud before the end of their tenure. The leader called on Pastor kubebe, a teacher in Santa Memorial College, to say the closing prayer.

Pastor Kubebe: O God, the creator of heaven and earth, the owner of everything visible and invisible. Your children were here to look for a way to break out from their respective chains, especially the chain of being a teacher in Kitoto. People see us as those who have taken a noble profession; teaching the ignorance to become enlightened. Many, through us, have been able to overcome most of their problems. But o Lord, see us here, looking wretched and hopeless. We hardly get help from people because they see us as working-class citizens. They do not know that we are in a chain that appears to be noble. Today, we have gathered to be free from this chain. We have come to say no to anything that will make us incapacitated. We have come to pursue a course of liberation. Father in heaven, we humbly pray that anything that shall stand as a hindrance to achieving this goal be destroyed. Touch the hearts of the leaders of Kitoto that they may understand what we are going through. Thank you, Lord, for answering our prayers.

All: Amen.

The members sang solidarity songs as they went out of the hall.

7

The Minister Meets the President

The teachers' union matter was the primary reason for the minister's visit to the president. The minister was in the president's reception an hour before the president's arrival. The president arrived at the office accompanied by other ministers, the secretary to Kitoto's government, the leader and a few members of the legislative arm of Kitoto's government. After the formal protocols, the president called on the minister of education to present his matter for discussion. The minister began his presentation in this way:

The minister: His Excellency, Sir, I'm here to brief you of the meeting I had with the leadership of the Teachers Union Association at the instance of the mandate given to me by this government. Before I continue, I wish to present the union's proposal to you for consideration (the minister submitted a filed document to the president). While going through it, Sir, permit me to briefly summarize the contents of the proposal for clearer understanding and for the benefit of everyone present.

His Excellency, Sir, the union leadership made a humble appeal to you for issues I consider needs urgent attention through my ministry. At the meeting there were talks about; salary increment and its prompt payment, sustainable welfare packages, study grants, suitable housing and pension schemes. They are soliciting your kind considerations, approval, and implementation of the under listed demands so presented. Your Excellency Sir, I wish you were there at that meeting to see how the union leadership poured their hearts; you would have seen their depression and hopelessness on their faces. Please Sir, on behalf of the union, I want to appeal to you to use your good office and look into their matter as some of the issues raised are indeed saddened. Thank you, Sir.

President: Thank you, my minister, for this briefing. So far, you have demonstrated beyond doubt that I did not make a mistake in appointing you into my cabinet. However, I know you do not understand how Kitoto politics is being played, and I cannot blame you for that. I think the leadership of the law-making body of Kitoto state will furnish you with our operational ethics. The information boss is here, he is very good at that too. I will want you to meet him personally after this meeting for indoctrination. I strongly believe that after meeting with him, you will know how to handle some of these matters anytime they are brought before you. At this point, let me allow the leader of the law-making body of Kitoto to educate you more on this. Though you are the education minister, but in this case, you must be educated by the cabal (all laugh).

Legislative leader: Thank you, Your Excellency! Mr Otuntu, my brother, as the president has rightly said, there is a way the administration of this state is run, which I'm very sure you are not aware of because you were not briefed. We suggested your name to His Excellency because we know you to be a very brilliant young man, and you are noted for being loyal to anybody who is a boss to you. I could recall when you were working under Mr Musaka, despite what was going on there. Many of us knew you were not carried along by Musaka, yet, you did not complain. His attitude did not make you disloyal to him until you jointly finished the tenure. That sincere sense of loyalty made some of us ask His Excellency to bring you into the circle. I know too well that you did not know why your name was suggested for the position. You may have thought that it was a miracle. Jesus in his first miracle turned water into wine. Both were liquid. He didn't turn water into stone. You can see the link that exists between wine and water? So for your name to have been mentioned, it means someone might have known you and suggested it.

Otuntu, my brother, let me make it known to you today that when you were given this portfolio, we planted some people in your ministry to monitor your official and unofficial activities. At least you are aware that some of the people working under you as aides got their appointments directly from members of the cabal, and they are answerable to this cabal and not to you.

Thus far, you have not been found wanting. The feedback we are getting from our foot soldiers is encouraging. It clearly shows your moral commitment to the discharge of your official duty.

However, it is unfortunate that your operational pattern makes you an *angel in an evil forest.* But how the angel will survive after eating the food from the evil forest is difficult to explain. I hope you know the table manner; one is not expected to talk while having food in the mouth. Your agitation for the teachers is a negation to this long-standing tradition and belief. That is why when His Excellency told us of your meeting with him, we begged him to allow us to be part of it so that we can use the medium to enlighten you on how the Kitoto government operates. We know how sensitive your ministry is to this government; if we allow you to mess up that department, either by an act of omission or commission, it will mean that the cabal is in a mess. That is why you see these faces here today.

The day has come for us to open your eyes to the reality of the government of Kitoto. There is this saying in philosophy that appearance is not reality. If I should bring this philosophy into our discussion, you will really understand that ideally, often, appearance is not reality. You see, people will always say, this Kitoto belongs to all of us. We cannot go out to argue this with them, but we know very well that it is not true that Kitoto belongs to everybody. Some people own Kitoto. Today, you are lucky to sit with some of the owners of Kitoto.

From today, get to know that Kitoto belongs to a few elites; they are the ones that decide the fate of Kitoto. His Excellency here is one of them. They are the ones that draw the template on how Kitoto should be run. It is not all of them that are in politics. Some are in the business sector; some are religious leaders, while some are the traditionalists with the extra power to manipulate the system to suit what political leaders want. The two most vital sectors are politics and business; we do not joke with these classes of people. So any policy or reformation we want to make, we must first consider the interest of the few elites in these two sectors. There is no way we can go against their interest; after all, they control a more significant portion of Kitoto's resources. They have been there before some of us came into power. They are still our bosses till tomorrow. To joke with them is like playing dice with your political fate.

After this meeting, I believe you will appreciate the fact that you are gradually coming closer to knowing how things are done in Kitoto. This is one of the opportunities many other politicians in Kitoto do not have, and they are seriously looking for such. I want to believe that you will not throw this golden opportunity into the mud. When your eyes are finally opened to see how things are done here, you will realize that in Kitoto, people do not protest because they want justice, but because their own interests are not accommodated. If you like, bring Satan to rule, you will be surprised to see a religious person becoming a campaign manager for his election if there is a promise of appointment. Do not be deceived; only those who are hungry and those whose interests are not protected go for protest and not those in the system, no matter how flawed the system is. This is Kitoto; our political system is peculiar. Other states may protest sincerely against bad governance, but here, any protest whatsoever is to protect one's personal interest. So you shouldn't allow protest or strike action of any union to make you fear. They can strike, but when we declare; "no work, no pay" that will be the end of the strike. Already Kitoto's law forbids anyone working with the government from engaging in any other meaningful business except farming. This is the law that helps to put all the workers in check; else they become wealthier than us and oppose many of our policies. As it is, they have limited power to challenge us. That law is our strength here in Kitoto. That is why anytime they strike; it is always for their stomach and not for the general good of the Kitotos.

Is there any time that teachers join doctors for protest or lawyers protesting in support of nurses? You will never see such in Kitoto. Everyone is fighting for his stomach. But while protesting, they will behave as if their protest is for the masses. When you call any of them for negotiation, you will understand whose interest they are protesting for. They will even negotiate against their own members if you promise them anything, no matter how insignificant the promise may be. Is that not what their successive leaders have been doing even before we came into power? Just relax your mind my young friend. Situation will take care of itself.

Let me give you a little tip, the cabal knows what to watch out for, whenever these hungry people take to the street in the name of protest or embarking on a strike action. First, we will want to know who they are. Secondly, we look out for the ones who have many followers, and thirdly, the ones who can endure threats from us. The ones with many followers and the ones that can withstand our intimidations are always the ones we put in our watch book.

Those we think are simple to buy over; we always call them over and give them small offices to occupy. We use them anytime we want to eliminate those that oppose our ruling style. The stubborn ones, we use force to silence them. This one has nothing to do with religion but with power. We must tell you all these things that you might know. If His Excellency should see your services as worthy of commendations, then he might consider it wise to bring you into the cabal. That is when you will understand that Kitoto belongs to very few influential individuals and not to all.

Here in the cabal; the only religion we recognize is our interest. We do not care which other religion you belong to outside of this group. We eat from the same plate and drink from the same cup here. It is only when we want their support that we talk about other religions. There is no other religion than the power to protect your interest. By now you should know that God is one, and any route you wish to approach him from, is your choice. However, they are powers in religion. At the mention of religion, a rational man can become irrational if he feels his religion is threatened. That is why we resort to religion anytime we want to get our controversial bills approved. We do not resort to appeal to religion because we are religious. No! That is not it. We appeal to religion anytime we want to achieve some goals.

I want to believe that His Excellency will deem it fit to draft you into this exalted cabal in due course. I see you as a very resourceful fellow whose services are needed to help us drive the dreams of the cabal in the educational sector. We know you have the power of words. I'm sure you know how exposed some of these teachers are. They are highly educated, and they always have good points to drive home their message, especially those in the ivory tower. Your level of comportment, intelligence, and good command of language put you in an advantageous position to dialogue defensively with them on matters that would be brought before you. Know this and know it well; that we needed you for a purpose. There were many other people canvassing for this position, because we know your worth, which was the reason the cabal decided to bring you into the fold.

We are not here to argue whether the treatment the teachers received from us is just or unjust. We all know that their monthly salary is not up to the money we use to fuel our cars in a day; we all know that. But you see, to me, that is their fate, and there is nothing we can do about it. In his concept of proportionate equality, a famous philosopher named Aristotle had said that the equals should be treated equally and unequal should be treated unequally. So no matter how the masses will cry, we cannot give them the same treatment we give to ourselves. We are the elites, and they are the masses. Can you now see the difference? We are the equals, and they are the unequal. If I should be raw with my words, I will say we are the free-born, and they are the slaves. In this sense, it is only when you belong to this family that you become a free-born; otherwise, you are a slave. But this is knowledge that must remain with us.

This is the ideology driving us. We dare not say this to their hearing, though it is the truth. The most important thing you should be thinking of for now is how you can protect yourself and your family from being attacked by them. By being a minister, you have made yourself an enemy to the masses; because you have already been perceived by them as a member of the cabal even when you are yet to be. To think that you can right the wrongs in this administration is like deciding to use an axe to clear grasses or a razor blade to cut an iroko tree. You can now see how difficult that can be. Or are you trying to rename a swimming pool a desert? My brother, these are difficult things to ever contemplate doing. There are things you don't need to bother yourself about.

The fortunate thing for the rest of us is that we have gradually made them to believe more in money than believing in integrity. Anyone among us who attempt to rise in their support instead of supporting us, we will close the looting window against the person. If you like, gather them on a holy mountain and tell them all the truth about what is going on in Kitoto, if you do not share money with them at the end of your speech, you would be seen as the most unsuccessful leader that Kitoto has ever produced. You know, we have studied them and understand who they like.

We know the language they will like to hear, which will end with some bundles of cash for them to share. In Kitoto, it is not the person who works to change the lousy structure that is a good leader; but he who has some money to share during the election.

Before now, I used to behave like you. I always go to the village even when the election season is far apart, and share the little money I have with them. Sometimes I sit with them to drink palm wine. I was tempted to believe that I was loved by the masses. On the day of my election, I got to know I was wasting my resources and time. My opponent, who did not visit the village even once before the election season, became the favored and the popular candidate because he could share just 100 tintua to each person, which I could not. My belief was that for being close to most of them, that I will win the election with ease. I lost the election to my opponent who did not even know the road to the village before the election. My brother, I have learnt my lesson. These days, I know when I can go to them.

A year to election's date is the right time to start picking their calls, attend their functions, and buy rice for them. That is the period to organize an empowerment program and target the influential people to give a slot or two. The empowerment program in Kitoto is not really for the poor. What will the poor and the less privilege and the disable do to give you victory at the poll? When you organize any of such programs, make sure the political thugs and some leaders are the beneficiaries. If there should be any disable among them; then that must come from the leaders that you trust. We understand all these things. Anything you do for them from your face year in office to the last month to the election, if you don't give them money during the election, forgets it; they will not vote for you.

This is not to say that the present system is good. No! We know too well that the system is terrible; that is why we do not allow our children to stay in Kitoto for long. Their schooling is better done outside Kitoto; after their graduation, we bring them back to continue from where we will stop. Many of them have indeed started getting in on our games, which is the more reason we must keep our children away from them, else they visit them with the anger that is actually meant for us.

Minister, my brother, there are many reasons we must allow the sleeping dog to lie. The last thing we will consider for now is increasing teachers' salaries. The little we have done to them thus far is enough, before you hand over a gun to your enemy to shoot you on the head. The truth is that the system of governance in Kitoto does not allow honest people to survive in it. So if you should stay, you must follow the system and not your conscience. If we should be sincere to ourselves, none of us can win in a free and fair election, even in our own communities. That is why we must always fight to ensure that the Election

Cooperation Council's (ECC) leadership is appointed by us. This is the body Kitoto uses to get what they want against the masses' decision. Though some of them are proving stubborn these days, we know how we will handle them in the next election. Arrangement is ongoing to relieve some of them of their appointment before the time. The loyal ones, we will keep.

It is true that the ECC cannot do all the magic that we want them to do independently, without the corroboration of those with chalk and pen; I mean the teachers. In an ideal society, I know teachers ought to be respected and their salary supposed to be reasonable enough to be appreciated. But if such an opportunity is given to them, they will soon be out of their chain, the noble chain that provides us with the power to use them at will.

If you could remember, the teachers in the ivory tower were not part of those conducting elections in Kitoto. It was those in the lower section of teaching that the Kitoto government used. Some people were of the view that the ones in the ivory tower will do better in protecting the interest of the masses. That was why they were drafted in. We tried to stop but we couldn't, because the person who was in charge of Kitoto was either not well schooled in the politics of Kitoto, or had wanted to change the culture of election in the state. Those who initiated the idea did not know that the inclusion of the senior men of the chalk would be to our advantage. They are now the ones we use to strike our deals.

The successive elections in Kitoto, you can see that they are the ones the ECC is using to do their jobs and always do it in line with our order. They do it not because they like us, but because they are poor. That is why they are always happy with the token we give to them. These people know who we are. They understand that the image of successive leadership of Kitoto has been marred with corruption, looting, laundry, and embezzlement, so giving them financial freedom will make them work against our goal; the goal of making Kitoto to remain our farm.

Now I want you to get my point! If we should increase their salary and other welfare packages, they will start living well and begin to decide for themselves. Once that is achieved, know that we and our children will be in trouble. We all know how our election used to go. If these people are well paid, many will not want to compromise during an election. This is the idea we got from different successive administrations in Kitoto, and it is the same thing going on throughout our neighboring Afitas states, of which Kitoto shares its root. This system is working for us. So to change it is detrimental to us.

Kitoto Announcer: Let me come in there, my eloquent leader! I want to draw the minister's attention to what we witnessed in the past two elections in Kitoto, how the most learned among them was used to manipulate elections in our favor. You should understand that the two things that can easily make a man of integrity turn away from his uprightness are money and women. Were these not the two things we used to lure these men with grey hairs from the holy seat of wisdom to become the mouthpiece that announced 69 as 96? All this was because we promised them some bundles of cash that they had not seen for their years in service.

You should know that when a man is hungry, even bitter leaves will taste sugary in his mouth. A small amount of money will appear as billions in his eyes. When a man is without money, he can even call a child "my boss". The truth is that the teachers of Kitoto are in chains, and we make it so because if we pay them well, they will never agree with us again during elections. Even if a few of them want to compromise, we will not have the kind of money they will demand.

President: You people have spoken brilliantly! My minister, I know you might feel disappointed at what you have heard, but I may tell you not to be. The administrative system of Kitoto has been structured so that even if St. Michael was to be brought down to rule, he will certainly not be able to function because the system was not designed for Saints. No Saint can survive in Kitoto as a leader unless he compromises the Saintly mentality for the prevailing system in Kitoto politics. The fact is that the people of Kitoto are not as corrupt as people think. It is the system that is corrupt. A Saint cannot survive under the present system of government in Kitoto. Kitoto people are nice, but the system is worse. If the system is changed, the people will be like angels. It is the bad system and what is going on in the state that makes the people afraid to help. Far back, the people were really their brother's keepers in the true sense of the word. But now, everyone is living in fear, because of too much distrust.

There are many lapses in Kitoto's constitution. Until certain things are changed in it, Kitoto will never make any significant growth. You see, the constitution gives me the power to decide who is to be the chief judge. I have the constitutional mandate to appoint whosoever as the Police boss. As the president, I have the power to appoint anybody into any of the offices. Yes! I am the president, vested with the power to do many things. I can use that same power to act in the right way or wrong; it all depends on what I want. But I am controlled by both internal and external forces. The cabal and other external forces always draw my attention to this excess power the constitution has given me as the president and then demand me to utilize the power in the interest of the cabal. You see? As the president, it is my place to ensure that the various interests of the cabal are protected. That was the first oath I took, the one on my swearing-in was just a ceremonial oath-taking. It is that of the cabal that count.

My dear, many of the things you see me do are against my conscience. But where is the place of conscience when an oath, agreement, and the demands of those who made me to become what I am are involved? Before my swearing in, the template of what the cabal wants was already with me. I begged them to add a little for myself. Yes! The power of Kitoto is in my hand, but it is controlled by the cabal. My dear minister, everyone is in the chain, theirs is noble while ours is a "golden chain." Anyway you look at it, it does not change the fact that we are in chains.

I actually meant everything I promised during my campaign. But when I was sworn in, the cabal members opened my eyes to see life and administration in Kitoto from a very new perspective. I cannot see life from the way the masses have presented to me. No! It must be from the horizon of the cabal.

For any leader or president of Kitoto to make any meaningful development, such a leader must first work towards the review of the constitution to cut down some of the powers of the president and other elected officers. But who will choose to spit out honey from his mouth to chew bitter leaf? That is where the problem lies. I can never be the one to take such a decision. The cabal will not even allow you to contemplate that unless you want to pay with your life before you finish such imagination. But how will anybody with proper sense wish himself death while living in affluent? Are there any of you here who are not living comfortably?

All: No one, no one (they all chorused)

President: Then what are we saying! I think what you should be contemplating on is how to ensure that the administrative power in Kitoto does not sneak out from our hands. One of the ways to do that is to go after those that may want to oppose our administrative style. Again, we must lure as many members as possible into our party. We shall open illegal means of wealth acquisition for them to make wealth. The unlawful means of getting wealth would be a chain we placed on their neck. Anytime they want to rise against us, we draw their attention to it. The stubborn one, we prosecute. Who among you are ignorant of what we passed through when we entered the system newly? They will give you documents to sign; and you will sign a different amount from what you actually collect. If you dare to question, they shout you down that you have no option than to keep quiet. That is the approach we adopt in dealing with those who claim to be holier than the Pope.

We shall also slow down the flow of cash as a controlling mechanism to avoid the masses from making wealth that will make them challenge our decisions. If we make the system unbearable for them and make them experience a little more hardship and suffering, they will not have the needed resources to fight us. This is to cripple any plans of revolution. We must intimidate them with killing and detention if they insist on embarking on any protest that might lead to revolution. We must do these things if we desire to remain in power. Let me tell you, as far as the world remains, there must be those who are poor and the ones that are rich. So hearing people complain of hardship, to me, is music whose rhythm will never change. It is natural that people must complain while others enjoy, so it does not bother me. No matter how they cry, it is their fate. It is their chain; they should not wish us to be the ones that help them to break out from their chains when we know their breakout will be to our own detriment. No one can give you peace, if you want peace, you fight for it! Peace cannot be bought in the market. How can we give them peace when we do not have peace ourselves? Please let everyone endure their chain, after all, there is no one without a chain.

No doubt, Kitoto has enough resources to make Kitoto one of the fastest-growing states in the world.

Still, the structure of our constitution has given us great opportunities to run the administration of Kitoto in a way that some selected individuals are favored, while others suffer, and we are comfortable with that. That is the irony of life. Nature makes it so and who am I to wrestle with nature?

That is why we keep telling you in this government never to allow the few individuals who claim to be holier than thou to have their way to sponsor any bill that can cause a change in the constitution on the floor of the house. Such an opportunity will certainly bring about a reformation in Kitoto; a reformation we are skeptical of. We do not want any reformation for now. It can be after our administration, but for now, no! But this we must stand firm to defend because by all indications, those pushing for it might succeed. That is why we must put some of your members in a closed watch.

I have already discussed with other cabal members not to allow those stubborn flies to have their ways back to the assembly in the next election. People like: Maryam, Bruta, Santutu, and a few others who are trying to expose the architectural blueprint of this administration, even when they know that their hands have been stained. None of them should be allowed to make it into the next assembly. We must go the extra mile to ensure that such people are not returning. If they like, let everybody vote for them, we will use the officials of ECC and the people in the noble chain (teachers) to finish them. It just takes a little bundle of money and a promise of cars; the deal will be sealed.

Announcer: That is the game, His Excellency! This is why we should not even consider what the teachers are demanding. But we should not also put it so straight to them that the Kitoto government will not oblige to their demands. The minister of education is here; we should make him promise them that their request would be granted. In this way, we will stop them from going further with their planned strike action or with anything that will disrupt the activities of the state. If they prove so stubborn, we call the union's leadership for settlement behind the scene. This is part of the strategies we have been using against other unions in Kitoto anytime their demands are brought before us.

Abrakachi: Everybody here has spoken well, but I want to make a little suggestion which I think will appear fair in the eyes of the people. I think we should adopt a "brocaded" approach in handling this matter. If not, we might not manage the boomerang effect of our decision.

Announcer: What is the brocaded approach? Please be plain.

Abrakachi: By brocading approach, I mean using a method that will make us appear true in our promises when actually we are not.

President: That sounds good! But what if it becomes that the promises are made in such a way that we cannot deny fulfilling them, especially as the elections is drawing near? What will become of us?

Abrakachi: It is simple! The government should accept to comply with all the demands made by the union. We will make the implementations look as if it would be immediate and in full scale. We shall deliberately form a committee to look at their demands. The committee will intentionally slow the process for months before it comes out with its report. The report should be drafted on salary increment alone when presented. This will provoke the union and make them insist on the inclusion of all their demands. The insistence will take another three to four months, if not more. The committee will finally come back with a comprehensive report. From there, the government through the minister of education will give them the reasons why they will not meet up with all of their demands simultaneously, and assure them that salary increment shall be a priority. This will cause another argument that will call for reconsideration. I know very well that the union will accept the offer of salary increment above others.

From here, the negotiation on the percentage will take another three months. If we can stage-manage the deal well, it will take us close to the election period. We have to make our planned scheming look so real that the people will be convinced of our seeming commitment to our promises.

Apart from the education minister, we have to use someone from the stronghold of our opposition party to address the aggrieved union members in defense of the government. The person must re-assure them of the government's willingness to attain to all their demands. However, we shall continue to give excuses with the assurance that all the promises we made shall be kept. If they embark on a demonstration or strike, we use our mercenaries to threaten them. In the case that it persists, we increase the salary by an insignificant amount. We shall find excuses for not implementing or fulfilling the promises maximally. That means we should promise big but do little. Let us make it look as if this present government has the interests of teachers at heart. The implementation should be done when the next election draws near. To me, the whole game should be championed by the education minister since that is his office, but we all must ensure it plays out well.

Education minister: Thank you, Mr President and other respected members present. I really appreciate the tutorial you have given me for free of charge, and it is now clear to me the direction the government of Kitoto is going, of which we, the members of the cabinet, ought to follow. But Sir, permit me to still appeal for your kind consideration. I have presented several things before you, and I beg that for the people not to say the government has failed completely, I think the government should at least fulfill three out of these demands. Even though we have a direction, we should not make it evident. I am also saying this in the good interest of His Excellency. At least we must have something to reference when we go out for campaigns.

To consider only salary is, to me, not too good. His Excellency, please reason with me.

Abrakachi: There is a point in what he is saying. I think we should approve a study grant for them. I know their management will make it difficult for some members to assess that they can make something out of it. We should also cause a tiny salary increment to give them hope that we will fulfill our promises. This will go a long way to protecting the image of this administration. It is my opinion, though.

President: I think this is a good suggestion. Minister, go back and hold a meeting with the union, inform them of the government's approval of all their demands, and then tell them that the implementation will start with the salary increment. Is that okay by you?

All: That is okay His Excellency! You are in order!! (They all respond).

The meeting ended, and everybody departed. Spy, a journalist quickly, ran to the minister for an interview. It was not more than 30 minutes after the meeting that the news headline reads; "Kitoto government has approved the implementation of all the demands made by Kitoto's teachers with immediate effect." The minister did not waste any time in calling for a meeting with the union members for briefing.

8

Minister's Meeting with the Teachers' Union

The meeting was scheduled for 9am on a Monday. The meeting witnessed the presence of all the executive members and other stakeholders of the union.

One could see a flash of hope on their faces. Their dresses portray a mixture of wealth and poverty, tragedy and comedy, and funny and sad experiences. The union leader came in, dressed in a well iron, starched faded shirt; resembling white and brown, on a khaki trouser with neatly polished unaligned black shoes. The secretary wore an oversized long sleeve shirt with a long tie. His black trouser only sustained on his waist by the support of a peeled brown belt.

Other members were not entirely different from them in terms of dressing. The unique thing about them all was that their clothes were clean, only that they were old and faded.

After the minister's briefing, there were mixed reactions. Some union members thought the union should strike until the so-called approved demands were implemented. In contrast, others believed that one week of grace be given to the government to redeem their promises. Should they fail; then the union will be left with no other option than to go on strike. For some time, the argument went on and on. The minister was dumbfounded; he tried to calm the tension but to no avail. Finally, the union leader sang solidarity song to gain their attention:

Union leader: If you see my children
All: Hosanna,

Union leader: Tell them say ooo
All: Hosanna,

Union leader: Suffer suffer,
All: Hosanna, teaching job.

Union leader: If you see my dear wife ooo,
All: Hosanna,

Union leader: Tell am say ooo,
All: Hosanna,

Union leader: Trouble go dey,
All: Hosanna, teaching job.

Union leader: If you see your husband
All: Hosanna

Union leader: Tell am say ooo,
All: Hosanna

Union leader: All is not well
All: Hosanna, teaching job.

Union leader: If you see president,
All: Hosanna,

Union leader: Tell am say ooo,
All: Hosanna,

Union leader: There is problem,
All: Hosanna, teaching job.

Union leader: If you see our colleagues,
All: Hosanna

Union leader: Let them know ooo,
All: Hosanna

Union leader: Level has changed,

All: Hosanna, teaching job.

Union leader: If you see my landlord,
All: Hosanna

Union leader: Tell am say ooo,
All: Hosanna,

Union leader: There is no rent,
All: Hosanna, teaching job.

As the leader continued in chanting the song, it was as if a new spirit of oneness was descending on them. Everyone was singing as if they prepared for any eventuality. "This was the union I knew when I joined the job." (One of the old teachers echoed). That was the first time the members witnessed the union secretary dance. The secretary uses a walking stick to support his movement because of the injury he sustained in his right leg while travelling for a union meeting in one of the cities in Kitoto. The injury which was badly treated because of lack of funds left him deformed.

After a brief moment of gyration, the union leader called for order and everywhere was quiet. The leader addressed the members in this way:

Union leader: Greatest Kitoto teachers!

All: Great!

Union leader: Ever conscious Kitoto teachers!

All: Great!

Union leader: I am so delighted by the cooperation you have demonstrated today in this meeting. Indeed, it has once again shown that there is a teachers' union in Kitoto. We have all heard what the minister has said; the promises made by the government of Kitoto to the union, but the contract gives me more pains than the solution we were expecting it to bring. The promise without knowing the actual time for the implementation is worse than not making a promise at all. Mr Minister, please tell this noble union when these promises will be fulfilled. The phrase "with immediate effect" aired on the news suggests even today. Should we expect the implementation today?

Minister: Ladies and gentlemen, as I always say, I feel and share in your pains and sufferings. Since my last meeting with you, I have not rested. I have met with different bodies and personalities on this same matter to see how your demands can be met. Thus far, my commitment to ensuring that this is done has yielded fruit. I urge you to bear with the government; I know things will be done in the soonest possible time.

All: When? Tell us how soon the soonest possible time is! (they retorted).

Minister: Let me assure you that your salary increment will come before the end of October this year. The government is working assiduously on the increment percentage, and I hope it would be an encouraging increment.

Asati: Thank you, Mr Minister Sir. I want to observe that you are only talking about salary increments of which we are not even sure of. How about other demands? Did the government not say anything about them? We are tired of these "brocading" promises. I think we should embark on an indefinite strike until the government is ready to respond to our demands because by all indications, the government is far from being ready to attend to our demands.

All: You are right! You are right!! You are right!!!

There was an uproar such that the minister could not control the situation anymore. Hence, the meeting was called to its disruptive end. One week after the unproductive meeting, the union leader called for an extraordinary executive meeting to seek the union's approval to declare a two-week warning strike in all schools. The request received a resounding welcome from all members, and immediately after the meeting, strike action was declared.

9

The Strike Period

After the two weeks' warning strike without any response from the government, an indefinite strike was further declared by the leadership of the union. The first month into the strike had passed without any reaction by Kitoto's government. The second month had equally passed, and not one statement was made by the government on the strike action apart from the memo with the title "no work, no pay" that was sent to the union by the minister of education informing the union of the government's resolve to stop the teachers' salary if they do not call off the strike. The third and fourth months passed and the enduring strike was still in limbo. It was in the fifth month that the government called the union for negotiation. Thus far, the negotiation was unproductive because of the insincerity on the part of Kitoto's government. Strike in Kitoto is common, but that of the teachers is a culture.

Before the negotiation, the minister had called some of the past leaders and stakeholders, including the present union leader for a settlement meeting. It was there that the minister promised to give the leaders one billion tintua to suspend the strike action, while they wait for the implementation of the approved demands. Many members were ready to key into the deal, but the union leader declined. The leader suggested that the discussion be suspended until other demands are made. Some stakeholders of the union were not happy with the leader's submission, but they could not push further. Some of them rather secretly negotiated with the minister for another meeting to discuss further on the settlement deal with the promise to use some of the executive members of the union to execute their plan.

After the settlement meeting, the minister once again called on the stakeholders including the union executive for further discussion. At the meeting, the minister and other stakeholders persuaded the union leader and his executive to call off the strike to open the floor for dialogue with the government. The minister disclosed the government readiness to pay their complete salary if the strike should be called off. But the leader insisted that he must reach back to the members before such a decision could be taken.

Just after the meeting, the union leader called for another extraordinary meeting of the union. The purpose was to inform the members the outcome of the two meetings he attended and to re-evaluate their strike option and the possible new approach to be adopted to ensure that all the demands are met. Bribing some of the union members has been a reoccurring tactic used by the government to destabilize the union's plans. The introduction of "no work, no pay" is another strategy adopted by the government to influence the decision of the union. Hunger will teach them a bitter lesson (the government reasons).

The "no work, no pay" strike action had entered its sixth month, no teacher received salary. Life was becoming unbearable. During this time, many male teachers had different degrees of issues in their respective families ranging from lack of food, medical care, and lack of funds for payment of utility bills.

House rent and inability to service loans collected from different financial institutions also tear some families apart. The experience had made some teachers resort to selling petty things in the streets to make ends meet. Some male teachers who were lucky to own cars started entering the roads with the cars in the evening with commercial intent just to raise money to feed their families. In the seventh month, many of them were already becoming full time commercial drivers. There was no difference between the men of noble profession and the professional taxi drivers in the street. It was a critical period for teachers whose only hope for feeding was their salary. Many of them went back to their respective villages. Those who were still familiar with the boundaries of their family lands located them for farming. Farming in itself is pleasant, but doing it out of frustration is disheartening.

The leaders who took part in the deal to end the strike used hunger as a reason to appeal to the rest of the members. They had agreed to make an appeal to the union leader and the members at the extraordinary meeting to end the strike. They had cautioned themselves to be careful, else their deal exposes.

When the information of the extraordinary meeting got to the members, everyone was anxious to know if the Kitoto government had finally agreed to their appeals. The members were ignorant of the outcome of the meetings with the minster, hence their curiosity was high. The meeting was slated for 10am, but before 9:30am, there was no space in the hall. The union leader and other executive members arrived the venue at about 9.50am. Everybody's eyes were fixed on the leader perhaps to read the outcome of the negotiation on his face. But how can that be possible from a man who has passed through terrible experiences on the account of lack of finance; for even his smile will look as if he is crying. No joy on the face of a man who is in great pain.

At the meeting, the union leader broke the sad news of the failure of the government to grant their desires. Members were so angry. Some of them were accusing the leadership of the union of compromise; some others accused the government, while the remaining members were confused on what to say. The leader called for calm and addressed the congress in this way:

Union Leader: My fellow comrades, I will not say that I'm confused to the extent of not knowing what to say.

As a leader, I must have what to tell you to bring hope to you all. We are here so that we can re-strategize our future. This unjustifiable chain on our necks must surely be broken. This is not a time to accuse or fight ourselves. Rather, it is the time to unite and fight this battle till we succeed. I am not angry that you accuse me of the things I am innocent of. That is not really my concern for now. My earnest concern is on what to do so as to change the narrative of teachers in Kitoto state. Since after the failed negotiation with the government, I have not rested; I have sent my mind to so many places in search of how to handle the situation. I have thought of going to court, but the question is; who owns the judges apart from them? In Kitoto, justice is not given; it is bought, especially when it is between the government of Kitoto and those it hunts. We do not even have the money to feed our families, where would we get the money to go to court! Some of the people I was relying on in this pursuit have disappointed and betrayed me, but I need not to talk about it for now.

I will always want any of our decisions to be collectively made. The minister has pleaded that we suspend the strike for the government to dialogue with us, but I clearly told them that I have no power to decide on that until I hear from you. Now I want to put it before you; should we suspend the strike for a dialogue or should we continue? The minister has promised that the five month's salaries would be paid if the strike action is suspended.

All: Let the strike continue!

Union leader: If we should continue with the strike option, how are we going to survive? This is the seventh month into the strike, we have not collected our salary; they stopped it because they know we cannot survive it. Truly! We are really in chains. As for me, I am ready to pursue this course to the end, my concern is you.

All: We are with you! Let the strike continue.

The struggle of the teachers to be free from chains in Kitoto is a fight that cannot end easily, unless the teachers themselves realize in thought and in actions that they ought to be noble in all their conduct especially during negotiations. But as it is, how noble are the teachers when the matter of negotiation and rigging in an election are involved? Between integrity and wealth, which one are the teachers always struggling to project? All these must be considered while the teachers are working to free themselves from the chain. What kind of punishment does the union give to their erring members irrespective of rank, especially when they betray the union? All these must be part of the things to be considered while strategizing on how to be free from chains.

The power for the teachers to free themselves from chains lies in their hands, and not really in the government of Kitoto's, as it appears to be. At the meeting, all the teachers were thinking on what to be done, Ifentem, one of the teachers that are noted for their high level of integrity when it has to do with official matters, indicated interest in making a suggestion. The union leader recognized him and called on him to speak. Ifentem held the floor of the house with the following words:

Ifentem: Great Kitoto teachers!

All: Great!

Ifentem: When you see masquerade dancing alone near the bush, know that the drummers are inside the bush drumming for him. For an extraordinary meeting of this kind to be called, even when we are still on strike, means there is something more important than just staying at home. To me this meeting should not be a gathering to discuss the government of Kitoto and what they have done to us. It should be a meeting for us to critically look at ourselves. We should use this meeting to know the areas we have gone astray as individuals and as a group. We should try to understand the reality of life; that it is difficult for someone to treat you more than what you truly deserve. Government will not treat us this way if some members of the union are not involved; either directly or indirectly to betray our trust. To some extent, we are a greater problem to ourselves than the government to us. If we want to stop thieves from entering our house, the first thing is to ensure that we lock our doors. If we fail to do so, our house will become their farm. Many things have happened but we pretend as if we are not aware. Before we think of shooting the sky, we must first and foremost crack the wall. Know that it is uncultured to eat an adult food with a baby's spoon.

Akana: What do you mean?

Ifentem: Good! Now listen. For about a decade now, during time for the elections, who do they employ as polling clerks in all the polling units? What about the people they select as the presiding officers and the ones they use as returning officers? Are we not the people? When people complain that elections are not free and fair, and that the elections were marred with rigging; who are the real people making the election not to be free and fair? Who superintendent the rigging, are we not the same people? Between the person who lobbied for election to be rigged in his favor and the person who actually rigged for him, who does the greater harm to the system?

How can a noble man stay in a hotel to write election results for someone who does not have anything to offer? Why should someone that calls his/herself noble want to negotiate how much he/she will collect from a political party or a candidate before he decides whether to go for an election or not? Tell me how teachers can be taken seriously when the most learned among us will mortgage our future and that of our children with the money that cannot take care of them for a week?

Are you not aware that some of the result sheets they gave us to announce were written by some illiterates among them? Most times their calculations do not tally with what is on record, yet they want us to do the magic of announcing without an error. Tell me why we will not be sweating in an air-conditioned room; when some of us would be trying to present six as if it is nine? Sometimes the valid vote-count is more than the total number of voters registered for the election. How on earth can that be possible! Yet, our so-called noble men would be sweating to defend the blunders. The government of Kitoto has carefully studied us and understands our weak points. That is why our suffering is ever persistent. For them to take us seriously, we must first be serious with the way we conduct ourselves as members of a union: a union that is supposed to be noble in all its dealings.

As Ifentem was still talking, some teachers became so sober as if they just finished confessing their mortal sins to a priest with a plea for mercy. One of the head teachers was seen wiping his eyes severally with a white handkerchief. He is amongst those who overturned a candidate's victory to another person in the past election. The hall was quiet that if a pin is dropped on the floor the sound could be heard. Ifentem did not conclude his speech when another teacher who is motivated by his insightful ideation interrupted with these words:

Santi: Ifentem you are the only one who has spoken the truth. Without doubt; we are the real enemies to ourselves and not the government per se. Why should we be struggling for an illegal meat-pie when a bag of rice is waiting for us as a right? We scramble to take part in an election not because of the desire to conduct a credible election that will change Kitoto's administrative system for the better, but because we want to present ourselves to be bribed by those who are desperate and had vowed to remain in power. Sometimes we are even the ones who initiate the idea of rigging; just because we are looking for money.

I know some of you will say it is because we are poor. But poverty is not a ticket to corruption. A noble man ought to be a man of integrity; whose character should speak volumes of his profession. Don't forget that the way you present yourself to the public. Is the same way you will be regarded? Are we not supposed to be the reformers? But today, we are struggling to be reformed. When Ifentem was talking, my eyes were filled with tears. I wept not because I am a perpetrator of the corrupt act we are complaining. I wept for seeing a drinker of whiskey being intoxicated with water. This is no time to say; "it is none of my business." Putting ourselves in the right tract is our business. The truth is that an injury to one is an injury to all. A destruction of a part is always a destruction of the whole. This is why we must call ourselves together. We must reform ourselves first. When we succeed in reforming ourselves, the Kitoto's government will not have any option than seeing us as the reformed, and then treat us in the manner we deserve.

Union leader: Then what should we do to achieve this?

Akana: Sir, we should make laws that will guide our conduct, especially on matters that concern Kitoto's elections and any negotiations that concern our union. Any of us that compromise in any of the elections or in the matter of the union, we should allow the law to take its cause no matter the position of the person. Such a person should be shown the way to his/her village. It is high time we bring sanity to our profession. This will make the government have respect for us as a union. Another election season is coming; our political leaders will begin to lobby us into their caucus. The reason for that is not for the love they have for us as teachers, but because they are preparing to use us for their bidding.

I am not saying we should not be part of their meetings. What I am saying is that we should go with our senses. When they offer you to be presiding officer, collation, or returning officer for the election, know that those politicians are up to something. The time we will refuse to compromise in an election; will be the very time the chain of humiliation and suffering enslaving us would be broken.

Whether the teachers would be free from their chains in the future or not, largely depends on their willingness to rebrand themselves, especially in matters of election and when they are pushing for implementation of any of their demands. The teachers' union should see the teaching profession as noble, and then allow the spirit of nobility to guide their affairs. Asking who is responsible for the sufferings of the teachers; the answer is that both the teachers and politicians are the culprits. Until teachers make some moves for their liberation; the politicians will not handle their matters with respect. While still waiting for such to be achieved, "the noble chain" remains their slogan.

www.ingramcontent.com/pod-product-compliance
Lightning Source LLC
Chambersburg PA
CBHW030128260626
47156CB00008B/2848